Fiction

Ed Jenkins.

max_ryan@Btconnect.com

Death Comes Hard
an original story by Garry Preece

Prologue typed up by Garry Preece

Part one typed up by Mike Hodges

Part two typed up by Joan Fletcher
and daughter Rebecca

Editing by Garry Preece

Completed on May 20th 2000

First edition printed at LULU.com August 2005

Second edition printed at LULU.com August 2005

Third edition printed at LULU.com September 18th 2005

Intro

This is the first long story I ever wrote, right back when I first hit double figures in my age. It has been through three drafts of major changes, and when it finally made it on to the computer, lots of small alterations have been made. I have to give thanks here to the people who kindly typed up my hand written work, no easy task given how bad my handwriting really is, thank you.

I have to say it is fitting that my first ever work is the first story to become published, I have dreamed to becoming a professional writer all my life, and this, I guess, is the next big step. I have over nine novel size stories completed now, and will slowly get them in print as well, something I never dreamed to be so easy only five years ago.

I also have to give credit to the Lulu publishing site for making this at all possible, they really give authors a great way to get started, and most importantly, get noticed.

This will hopefully be the last edition, I really need to get work proofread before I publish it. Hopefully there aren't too many mistakes left in the book.

Finally, I would like any readers to know that later works by me will be under my pen name Edward Jenkins.

Now the Intro is over, get reading, and most importantly have fun with this story, it's not my best work, but it is my first, and this story is the one that started my passion for the pen.

Garry Preece

4

DEATH COMES HARD

Prologue

A gunshot fired.

The hostages became suddenly silent in fear as the security guard fell to the floor limp, his brains covering the sidewall.

"Anyone else want to try being a hero?" the gang leader said, smoke drifting from the nozzle of the 45 calibre in his hand, "no, good, now get back to filling the bags or I'll repaint another wall!"

Five bank robbers, all armed and each wearing a balaclava, watched impatiently as the cashiers filled the bags with money as quickly as their shaking hands would allow.

The Bank door opened.

Spinning at the sound, the leader of the group and two others faced the newcomers, they took a split second to observe them before firing.

A young, hysterical, female cashier screamed as she watched everything develop in a nightmarish slow motion.

Two teenage boys had entered unaware of the bank robbery in progress and had reacted even quicker than the robbers themselves.

She watched the two boys' dive either side of the entranceway to avoid the oncoming bullets, which shattered the glass behind.

One teenager, wearing glasses, quickly found his feet and attacked the gunman standing closest to him. He kicked the gun out of the man's hands and smashed his fist into the side of his face with bone breaking strength. The boy, in his late teens', and dressed in blue jeans and white, open top shirt, was soon battling the next gunmen behind.

6

The other teenager, who had dived to the left, was on his feet almost as quickly and was the mirror image of the other he had entered with. The second gunmen he fought coming victim to a double kick to the chest.

When his second opponent was down, the teenager with the glasses turned on the man in the centre of the room, but without warning a bullet struck him in the chest and sent him tumbling backwards over a table. The man, who had killed the security guard, turned to shoot the other teenager but was just in time to receive a fist full of rage. A volley of punches, fed by anger, struck the man in the face over and over again, until he fell into the world of the unconscious on to the floor, blood pouring from the multiple wounds on his face.

Checking quickly to make sure none of the robbers posed a threat any more, the teenager ran over to the table where the other had landed.

"Ed! You OK?" he said as he approached.

"I will be," came the reply from the other side, "Mike did we win?"

"Would I be talking to you if we didn't."

The young women who had screamed fainted.

8

DEATH COMES HARD

Part 1

"How you feeling?" Michael asked, sitting down.

"Better every day" Edward replied, he had been in hospital for almost a week now and it still felt like a dream, the bank robbers, getting shot, a glimpse of the surgery. The pain had been immense, he looked up at his friend and quickly became concerned, "Mike, you look troubled, what's up?"

"You think you can handle some bad news?"

"You know I prefer to have bad news sooner rather than later."

"Well, you're not the only person I came here to visit." Michael took a deep breath and slowly let it out before continuing, "Kate was knocked down in a hit and run."

Edward's jaw dropped,

"What?"

"It happened yesterday, she only just got out of surgery a few hours ago."

"How bad?"

"Very, she might lose all feeling in her right arm, it was smashed. Her left lung was also badly damaged, along with five broken ribs, a fractured pelvis, lots of cuts and bruises, AND THE DOCS SAID SHE WAS LUCKY!" Michael said in anger.

"Hey Mike, calm down."

A few moments passed in silence. Edward remembered the first day Kate and Mike had gone out together, it was almost a year ago now, and

10

Edward had known from the start that it was love. There was no doubting that now.

"What are you sitting there for?" he finally said, "Kate needs you more than I do."

Michael gave him a look of thanks before getting up. Walking down the long corridor of the ward with beds flanking him on either side suddenly kindled the image of a funeral in his mind. He realised that in the space of less than a week he had come close to losing his best friend and the first girl he knew he truly loved. Life would never be the same without them and he probably wouldn't be able to continue himself. With this conclusion in his mind he considered that death wasn't hard on the dying it was in fact hard on the ones who continued to live.

He passed through the clean, white double doors at the end of the corridor and followed the floor markings to the intensive care area. Kate would be staying there for a few days before she could be moved to the general ward. He was so withdrawn in his own thoughts that it wasn't until he actually walked into the trainee nurse that he noticed her.

"Sorry" he said as he came to his senses.

"It's okay." The young trainee looked at him; "It's Michael isn't it?"

He looked at the nurse again and then recognised her; Edward had introduced her to him after he had plucked up the courage to finally ask her out the day before. Michael had always thought that hospital romance was just fiction, until the nurse had said yes.

"Sally, yes, it is."

"You look half dead." Noticing his pale complexion and red eyes, "You're not ill are you?"

"No, but I wish I was, I just haven't had any sleep, that's all."

"What happened?" She hadn't known Michael long, but she knew he wasn't his normal humours self.

"We both have dates on hold now." Michael said, "My girlfriend's in intensive care."

Sally tried hard to control her emotions; being a nurse it was one of the hardest and most important of tasks to achieve.

"How is she?"

"Stable, as far as I know, I'm just going up to see her."

"I could walk with you if you'd like, make sure you don't walk into anyone else."

"No, it's okay, besides, you're probably busy."

"Actually I just finished my shift."

"Well in that case, I suggest you go and visit Ed. I left him all alone and he hasn't any other visitors today."

"As long as you're sure you're okay." Sally checked.

"I'm fine, believe me."

"It's no good trying to lie to a nurse, but if you'd rather be alone, I'll go keep Edward company. Just make sure you get to Kate without having any more accidents."

Michael nodded and managed half a smile before turning and continuing on his way. After reaching the intensive care ward he quickly found a nurse to direct him to Kate's cubicle and he was soon standing at the foot of her bed.

He looked on at her beauty as he had done many times in the past, and as always he was transfixed. Her long wild black hair framed her face, high cheekbones and rich, red lips. Elegant sharp nose, long eyelashes and, although her eyelids were currently closed, he knew he could always get lost in her deep brown eyes.

12

He prayed that he would get the chance to look into her eyes again, though she was said to be stable the doctors had not been able to wake her. She was in a coma, and it was now that Michael noticed the mass of equipment also in the cubicle with her.

The heart monitor echoed her heartbeats, the only sound Michael could hear. The breathalator was close by and ready for use if it was needed, though Kate had a badly damaged lung, the other was strong enough and still working correctly. She did not need help to breathe and the doctors had said that this was a great sign. Drips and equipment he didn't recognise were either connected to her body or set to one side if needed.

"Excuse me sir, but visiting hours ended ten minutes ago."

Michael turned to face the senior nurse.

"I only just got here."

"Actually you've been standing in that same spot for over an hour. I noticed you arrive and felt you needed to be alone."

Michael looked up from his watch and tried a smile; "I thought time only went quickly if you were having fun."

"That's not always the case." The nurse assured, "I can let you stay a little longer."

"No, it's okay, if I don't leave now, I never will."

Michael walked round the side of the bed and bent over, kissing Kate on the forehead before rising.

"See you later Kate."

He turned and started to walk away before coming to a sudden stop.

"What's wrong?" the nurse asked.

Before he could answer he heard a voice, which filled his heart with joy.

"That wasn't much of a kiss, and where am I?" Kate's voice was very weak and almost inaudible.

He turned and looked into Kate's deep brown eyes, which looked right back at him, and all he could do was smile.

***

Kate recovered in leaps and bounds and within a week was moved to the general ward, even though her one lung was still not working at full strength, but it was working and with it her chances of surviving her ordeal were that much higher.

"Visiting hour just seems to go so quick." Michael said, rising from Kate's bedside, giving her a kiss and a gentle hug.

"Look on the bright side, the quicker they go, the quicker I'll be out of here and back home." Kate said returning his kiss.

"Hi, I just finished my shift, any chance of a lift?"

Michael turned to face Sally, the young trainee nurse that had fallen head over heels in love with his best friend Edward, who was in the other ward.

"Not a problem."

"Great." Sally said and blushed seeing Michael and Kate in an embrace; "I didn't interrupt anything did I?"

"We were just saying goodbye, that's all." Kate said as she kissed Michael again before releasing him so he could stand. "See you tomorrow Mikey."

"Oh, you will."

"And I'll see you in the morning I guess," Kate continued, nodding to Sally who had become a good friend.

"Well, I do work here."

"Just make sure the water's not cold."

"Excuse me?" Michael said confused.

"I'll be giving Kate a bath tomorrow, get her nice and clean after all your slobbering over each other." Sally explained.

"Hey, now that's a job I should be doing."

"You'll get your chance when I'm home." Kate said, "Now get out of here before the matron kicks you out. Again."

Michael smiled; "Okay, I'm going, I'm going. See you tomorrow."

"You better," Kate smiled.

"See you Kate."

"Bye Sal."

Michael and Sally walked down the ward, Michael turning every so often to blow a kiss back to Kate, who watched him until the double doors closed behind them. She couldn't wait to leave the hospital in Michael's arms, whenever he visited she felt truly alive.

She spent an hour or so solving some logic problems in her puzzle book. She wasn't ready for sleep yet, still on a high after Michael's visit, as always. She was just about to complete a puzzle she had not long started when a shadow fell over her book. Looking up, the smile she wore grew larger.

"Edward." She grinned.

"Hi Kate." Edward replied.

"But I though visiting hours had ended."

"They have, but not for fellow patients."

Edward sat down in the chair Michael had vacated just an hour ago.

"So Kate, how you feeling?" He asked.

"Better every day, but I'll be glad to get out of here. Actually I thought you would have been discharged by now."

"To be honest, I'm going home tomorrow, but…" Edward stopped, not quite knowing how to go on.

"But what?" Kate asked, "You should be happy you're going home, you'll finally be able to take Sally out on a proper date."

"Not if I don't save her first." Edward said.

Kate stopped and let Edward's words sink in, she had a horrible feeling this wasn't just a social call; "Why would you have to save her?" She asked slowly, confusion in her voice.

"Kate," Edward said with a sigh, and tried a half smile; "to think, the first time I get to visit you I have bad news." His attempted smile left his face, as his expression became serious. "You're the only person I know I can trust."

"I'm glad you think so, but I can't keep secrets from Michael."

"You don't have to. He's in the same boat as Sally."

"Are you trying to tell me he and Sally have fallen in love while we were stuck here in hospital?" Kate's anger was evident in her voice, though she tried to keep calm.

"No." Edward said, shaking his head; "It's nothing like that, it's…" Edward took a deep breath and let it out slowly before continuing. "They have both been kidnapped, it appears that a member of the gang who attempted to rob the bank had an older brother, bent on revenge."

"But Sally wasn't involved." Realisation struck. "Do you think Michael's still alive?"

"Easy Kate, I doubt anything's happened to him yet. They grabbed Sally to get me, a sort of exchange, my life for hers. I don't think Michael will be harmed until they have me. That's how revenge types like to work. Take it out on all parties involved at the same time."

"You have to call the police, you can't..."

"Kate, calm down, if I call the police both Michael and Sally die. I don't want that to happen. I've not had long to figure out a full proof plan, but I'm not waiting to hand myself over to them either."

Kate wiped tears from her eyes before looking at Edward. "You said you hadn't got a full proof plan. So does that mean you've got a plan?"

"I suppose. I've been instructed to go to a warehouse tomorrow afternoon. I plan on going tonight, and I'm going to need your help."

"Anything."

"Think you can drive?"

"With a broken arm? I don't know, I guess I could if you hold the wheel while I change gear."

"Good."

"Where do we get a car?"

"I'm going to have to steal one from the car park, I'll be able to get it going but not being able to drive does have it's drawbacks."

"You're almost nineteen now, you should have started taking lessons ages ago."

"I didn't see the point, I don't need a car so why waste the money?"

"Okay look, you're going to have to help me to the car, I can walk but I tire quickly."

"That won't be the problem." He sighed; "They grabbed Mike and Sal as they left the hospital, and they added in this letter," Edward showed Kate a crumpled piece of paper, "Which was forced into my hand by someone rushing past. They say they have the place watched."

"That's why you can't trust anyone else." It was a statement rather than a question.

"We have to make it look like we're still in our beds, in case someone checks up on us, otherwise we'll lose our surprise attack."

"What if something goes wrong? We have to leave some sort of message for our family and friends."

"I know, I've already made a small note, explaining what I'm trying to do and why. I've even added a goodbye note if something goes wrong. I suggest you do the same. On the final round and lights out, be ready. We leave at one o'clock."

"Edward, even if something does go wrong, thanks for counting me in. I wouldn't want to be left behind."

"Just be ready at one. Then we'll go rescue our friends."

***

One o'clock came and Kate was sat on the floor, already out of the bed she had made up to look occupied, a task made easier, for the woman in the bed next to her wore a wig which looked like her own hair. She had managed to get changed under the covers into more suitable clothes, a pair of blue jeans and a baggy black T-shirt, a simple task that her bandaged arm made a real struggle.

18

Time passed.

Looking at her watch she could see that Edward was already five minutes late and she began to worry something had already gone wrong. She gave him a bit longer, and just as she decided to go look for him, Edward appeared.

"What took you so long?" Kate whispered as Edward crouched down next to her.

"Almost ran into the night nurse, had to lie low 'til she had gone. I think she's a bit early with her rounds."

Kate looked into Edward's blue/grey eyes,

"How are we getting out of the hospital? We can't just walk out of the front door," she whispered.

"I know, but this isn't a prison, we're leaving by a window. The one near the stairs is out of sight and quite large."

"Wait a minute, walking I can do - just, but I'm not going to be able to go climbing out of windows in my condition."

"Don't worry, I'll carry you out, besides, were on the ground floor already. Once outside we have to stick to the shadows to reach the car park. There should be at least one car without an alarm. There's nothing to it."

"I'll agree with you when we're driving away from here, not before."

"Okay, right, I think the coast is clear, let's go. Stay close." Edward said as he led the way.

He wore black jogging bottoms, a dark blue 'T' shirt and black jacket; a plain black baseball cap covered his dark hair.

Kate noticed then that he carried his trainers, his bare feet on the smooth, tiled floor made no sound as he walked. Not wanting to spoil the silence, Kate removed her own trainers before following.

She found the floor hard and cold to her bare feet, but it actually felt quite pleasant. They reached the stairs without incident, and Edward unlocked and opened the large bay window. He half stepped through before picking Kate up in his arms and carefully placing her on the ground outside with almost no effort. He then followed her out and closed the window.

"Great." Kate whispered, "It's raining, and my feet are now as sodden as the grass I'm standing on."

"Stop complaining, it's only drizzle."

"Well." She said, taking a breath, "This drizzle is making it harder for me to breathe. I'm not out of breath yet, but if I walk all the way to the car park in this I don't think I'll be in any condition to drive. I'm having more doubts about this plan."

"Would you rather stay behind?"

"No way!" Kate almost shouted.

Edward put up his hands, mockingly fending her off. "I was only kidding, I'll carry you to the car, besides, you don't weigh much anyway."

"I'll take that as a compliment."

"I'm glad."

Edward picked Kate back up and headed towards the car park at a gentle trot.

They soon reached it and found they wouldn't have to break into a car. There was one already running, with the door open. The driver had just got out to dash into the hospital after his pregnant wife. The small man was so preoccupied that he completely forgot about his car. There weren't many other people about, only a handful of nurses just inside the accident and emergency block who could be seen in reception.

Taking this great opportunity, Edward ran over to the car and placed Kate in the driver's side before shutting the door and getting in the passenger side.

"This was a good bit of luck." Kate said.

"Yeah, I reckon, but let's not hang around 'til he remembers and gets back."

"Don't worry, the car's the last thing on his mind right now." Kate said, adjusting the seat. "I'll need you to hold the wheel when I say, and only when I say." She sighed, "Strange luck, if my left arm had been broken instead, I wouldn't be able to do this."

Putting the car in gear, she slowly pulled away from the hospital.

The owner of the car was so overjoyed with his new baby son that the car wasn't noticed missing until the following night.

***

Michael found himself thrown back into the darkened room the kidnappers were using as a makeshift cell. Sally was soon by his side and attempting to patch up the number of cuts and slashes he had received from the going over the kidnappers had given him.

"Five against one." He said, taking deep breaths "Is not fair." He was still winded and found talking hard. "Especially if you're tied up."

"Take it easy Mike, I want to check nothing's broken before you get up." Sally said.

Michael ignored her request, and stood up. His dark brown hair was messed up, and some of it fell over his left eye, though it was his right, which was bruised and swollen. He didn't look too pretty just now, and his wry smile had been long gone.

"The only thing broken is my hope of getting us out of here alive." Michael stopped and considered something before continuing, "And possibly my jaw."

"If you don't let me patch up those cuts they'll go septic. I heard one of them mention Edward." She said as Michael allowed her to continue cleaning his wounds. "I think they want him so they can kill you together to satisfy their egos. They're using us as bait and I'm certain he'll try something foolish."

"Yeah, probably end up getting all of us killed. Oh no."

"What?"

"If they sent word to him to come alone, he must be certain that someone's watching him, a doctor, nurse, fellow patient."

"So?"

"So the only one he can truly trust would be Kate. No, he wouldn't get her involved would he?"

"I don't know, I've not known him as long as you, but I doubt he'd try and rescue us alone."

"Yeah, right, he isn't that suicidal."

"Think you'll be able to second guess him and be ready when he arrives?"

"I don't know, but he'll most likely come either tonight, or early morning. I think we've been here for a few hours and since we were grabbed around ten o'clock, I reckon, since I no longer have a watch, that it's around midnight."

"So you think he'll get here in a few hours time then?"

"Maybe even less, the quicker he acts, the more surprise he'll have."

22

"I hope he's got a good plan." Sally said as she continued to patch up Michael's many wounds.

***

A jet-black mini with racing green stripes, removable top and alloy wheels pulled up outside a disused warehouse. The lights had been turned off a long time ago.

"They're being held somewhere in that building." Edward said.

"This mini's been upgraded to racing spec. We'd better not damage it. The owner must love this car."

"Don't worry, he'll get it back in one piece. I hope. You stay here as backup, keep the engine running and be ready to make a quick getaway."

"Right and you?"

"I'm going in, I hope I can go in and get them out without being seen."

"And if something goes wrong?"

"When the action starts it's going to get messy very quickly. Be ready to improvise if necessary."

"You know, we could spend a little bit of time planning this a bit more, it's only two o'clock."

"To be honest, I hate over planning. Let's keep this neat and simple."

"Just be careful out there, and try to bring my Mikey out in one piece."

"No worries." Edward said, and left the small car.

The night was cold and fresh. As Edward made his way
swiftly toward the building he felt the hairs on the back of his neck rise.
There was something else in the air tonight, something electric. He was
soon by the lone building, and these strange feelings were quickly
forgotten. He slowly checked through the window, three men were sat
over a table playing cards. This was the only room with light, and he
couldn't see any other activity. He noticed the large double doors
opened into this room and there were four more doors leading deeper
into the warehouse.

Deciding against the direct approach, he took to the fire escape and
worked his way to the next floor. The window was open, but barred; he
wasn't going in that way. Continuing up the red painted fire escape he
passed more floors before reaching the roof. He'd have to break in
through a skylight, and did just that, smashing the thin glass into an
empty room.

Once inside, he opened a door ajar and looked through. Darkness
greeted him and he thought it would be more of a blessing than a
hindrance to his search. Edward entered the corridor and began looking
for his friends.

***

Sally finished patching up Michael's wounds as good as she was able
with the materials to hand, though neither her nor Michael had tops to
wear now. She had ripped them up and used both as bandages. She was
now wearing only her skirt and white sports bra; Michael had jeans and
patches of bandage. Both of them were barefoot, the kidnappers having
taken their shoes to discourage any attempt to escape.

"I'm sure I heard something. Somewhere above us I think." Sally said.

"Well, I didn't, but just in case, we'd better get ready for a fight. At
least my jaw isn't broken."

"I didn't say it wasn't broken, it doesn't feel broken, but it still could be that bad. At the very least I reckon it's fractured."

"As long as it won't affect my kissing."

"It will if you get hit in the face any more. Just be careful if any fighting starts."

"Well, it helps being a brown belt in Karate."

"That it does, but a third Dan in ju-jitsu is slightly better." Sally said enjoying the look of disbelief on Michael's face. "I don't think staring suits you."

"It's, well, I mean, aren't you just a bit young to be a third Dan?"

"I reached black belt at just under 13. I'm almost 19 now, I've been a black belt for six years."

"So why are you training to be a nurse? You could teach at that level."

"I don't want to turn something I enjoy into a career. It takes the buzz out of it."

"Well, that's altered my plans a bit." Michael sighed.

"Oh?"

"I was going to charge out first when the door opens, but I guess, as you're more skilled than I, ladies first." Michael said, showing her the door.

"Thanks, I think." Sally said, biting her lower lip.

***

Kate sat patiently in the Mini; she hadn't left the engine running as Edward had requested, because she felt it would draw too much attention. She checked the time. Only ten minutes had passed, though it seemed much longer. Just as she thought Edward would make a clean getaway, all hell broke loose.

As she watched the building, the window directly above the one on the ground floor smashed outward, and the limp silhouette of a body fell to the floor. She heard shouts come from the building and although she couldn't make out the words, she knew that Edward's presence was now known. She started the engine and put the car in gear. She would give Edward a few minutes to reach the ground floor before smashing her way through the double doors. She only hoped the doors were not as strong as they looked, and made a silent apology to the mini's owner for what she was about to do to his car.

***

Sally stood in front of the door to their temporary cell. She could hear sounds of a struggle outside, and she unconsciously brushed her shoulder long blond hair behind her ear, as she got ready to fight. Twice the door was knocked inward by something and then the sound of a breaking window was followed by a silence so complete, that Sally could even hear her own breathing. The door lock clicked open and Sally noticed she was holding her breath. As the door slowly swung outwards, she kicked, feeling this would be their one chance of escape. Her foot pushed the door hard into a man; knocking him back into the darkened hallway, moonlight providing little illumination through the broken window. She ran through the doorway and jumped onto her fallen opponent, only to be thrown off in one simple movement. She stood and turned as she landed, and as she faced her already standing opponent a smile covered her face.

"I am supposed to be rescuing you, you know." Edward said as he looked into sally's bright green eyes, the moonlight making her already pale skin look white.

"You could have said something earlier." Sally replied as she wrapped her arms around him.

"Where's Michael?" Edward asked as their kiss ended.

"Right behind you." Michael said. "I do hope you have a plan for getting out?"

"Not really, my plan was a bit simple. Get in, find you, get out."

"You call that a plan?" Michael said.

"It's worked so far. Kate's waiting outside in a car, come on."

Michael raised an eyebrow. "Car?"

"We, er, stole one. But we'll give it back when we're finished with it," Edward promised.

"We'd better make a move, the way they're shouting downstairs, they must know something's up." Sally said.

"Quickest way out?" Michael asked.

"The window, but we're two storeys high, so it looks like the stairs."

"Up or down?" Sally said.

"Down. If we go up we're trapped, the fire escape wasn't guarded coming in, but it will be going out." Edward said.

"Well, the quicker we go, the quicker we get out of here."

They ran down the hallway and Edward kicked the door open, sending the man on the other side tumbling down the first part of the stairway. The room they entered was the same one Edward had seen from the outside, though then he hadn't realised it was two storeys high. The stairs they had come out on ran above the window he had looked through. The double doors he knew led outside were on the other side of the room straight ahead. A simple table sat at the far side of the room to their right, though the chairs around it were no longer occupied. The men originally in the room when he had looked in were no longer alone, and a quick count gave the number now as seventeen. They quickly started down the steps; to turn round now would be like giving in. Sally was in front and as she made the second flight an armed man fired on her with an automatic, taking her legs from under her and causing her to fall the rest of the way screaming in pain. Edward was right behind, and felt a bullet hit him in the side, though it didn't slow him down as he ran after the one he loved.

As Michael reached the small platform, the dark haired man who had been knocked down grabbed his feet and sent him over the rail. Michael hit the floor hard, banging his head, and as his eyes focused he found the barrel of a gun in his face. He glanced to his left and could see Edward at Sally's side, near the base of the stairs where more gunmen stood over them as well.

They hadn't made it.

Michael waited for the end. He closed his eyes and heard a massive bang, but it wasn't the sound of a gun firing. It was the sound made by a small black mini smashing through the large double doors to the warehouse.

Michael's eyes flicked open and he grabbed the gun away from the man standing over him and kicked upwards. Michael was too focussed to cringe in sympathy for his attacker. He flipped onto his feet and used the man's bent form to flip over his back and kick two more opponents down. He ran for the car, kicking or pushing away anyone who got in the way.

Kate had got out of the car to help Sally get in the back while Edward used anything he grabbed as a weapon to fight off his opponents. Even the men's own bodies as he flung them into others.

Michael quickly reached the car, rolled over its bonnet to reach the other side, and jumped in the drivers seat.

"Edward! Stop playing!" He shouted as he put the car in gear, knocking down more enemies.

28

Kate had only just made it into the back with Sally before the car started to move. She was desperately trying to stop the bleeding from the many bullet wounds in Sally's legs, and hadn't noticed Mikey get in the car.

Edward heard Michael's call, and as the mini came past him, jumped into the passenger's side, shutting the door just moments before they drove out through the hole Kate had made only moments before.

Michael felt the back of his head, his hair thick with blood, he had hit the ground hard but he felt no pain from the new wound. Only adrenaline ran through his veins now, pure adrenaline, although his jaw still pained him.

"They're giving chase." Kate said, looking behind. "And Sally's losing blood fast, we need to get to a hospital."

"We'll have to lose those guys first." Edward said, already weak with blood loss as well. His second gunshot wound was far more fatal than the first.

"Don't worry about me, I've got time yet." Sally said, trying to hide the pain in her voice.

"Just hold on, this mini maybe racing spec' but we wont outrun them." Michael said

He was proved right too quickly as one of the following cars pulled along side and rammed into the driver's side of the mini.

"Dam son of a...."Michael started, but a second collision interrupted him.

The mini raced the car along side around five bends, taking hits when the other driver was able, before a junction came into view. The turning was to Michael's right, and he had an idea. Checking his mirrors he could see the other chasing car a little way back.

"Hold on!" He shouted, and hit the brakes.

The car along side suddenly gained the lead, and opened the door to the turning. Spinning the wheel, Michael hit the accelerator again and the black mini, now with large dents in its side, turned towards the new road. It went wide, cutting over a grass covered corner, but made it, leaving the pursuing cars in its wake.

His passengers were shaken up a bit, but he enjoyed the reckless speed he was driving and felt it was even more fun cross-country.

"We won't be able to stay ahead for long, any idea where we are?" Edward said.

"None," Michael said, "it wasn't as if I had the time to look at the sign post."

"They're catching up again!" Kate said as she continued to look out the back window.

Sure enough two sets of headlights came speeding out of the darkness behind, and Michael had to blink the spots from his eyes, as he was dazzled,

"Dam it!" he said, "I thought I bought us more time than that."

The pursuing cars were right back up to the mini's bumper in no time, and the one who had been ramming before shunted the back.

"The owner is going to be pissed when we give him his car back." Michael said.

A bend came up on the road and before Michael could turn in, the car behind shunted him again and sent the mini out of Michael's control.

The black mini went over the grass hill at the bend, and down the embankment of a motorway.

"Lucky there aren't many cars about." Edward said as Michael wove his way through what little traffic there was as he regained control of the car and proceeded to accelerate.

"I'm just glad we're going the right way. Are they following?"

"Yeah." Kate said subdued, as she watched their pursuers drive down the embankment and onto the motorway.

"There's never a copper when you need one." Edward said.

"At this hour in the morning I'm not surprised." Kate said.

"At least it's started to brighten up a bit." Sally added, her voice weak with blood loss.

"Ah…" Michael said.

"What?" Edward asked, worried.

"Due to the fact we are now on a motorway, we have no advantage at all." He continued, as one of their pursuers quickly passed them, "He's going to block the junction."

"How far to the next one?" Kate asked

"About seven miles, then we have to get back." Michael said and glanced back to Sally. "You won't last that long." He said matter-of-fact and looked to Edward before his eyes settled back on the road. "And neither will you."

"Couldn't you go around the blockage?"

"No, if we try, the car behind will pin us in, and it would be over."

"Any ideas Mikey?" Kate asked biting her lower lip.

Edward saw the bridge coming up in the distance. Not far in front was one other vehicle, an empty transport vehicle, with the ramps poorly supported. An idea hit.

"Mike, get behind that lorry." He said, fingering an automatic gun that he had taken in the fight earlier.

"What's the plan?"

Edward wound down the window, and leaned out with the weapon.

"Er… I hope you're not…"

Michael was interrupted as Edward fired the machine gun at the lorry. His aim wasn't perfect, but with the constant spray of bullets he managed to sever the chain holding the two ramps in place. While he was half out of the car, a passenger in the chasing car took advantage of a clear shot and fired on Edward, the bullet hitting him in the small of the back, and piercing his heart.

But the wound didn't kill him. Edward fell back into his seat, but did not have the strength to refasten his seatbelt; the gun he had used had fallen from his hands, but thankfully was no longer needed.

"Okay Mike." Edward managed. "Now we have a ramp."

"It's moving."

Edward managed to smile and let out half a laugh. "Just makes it a more interesting story to tell our future kids."

"I can't believe we're doing this." Michael said, as he pressed the accelerator pedal to the floor. He knew any other way would be too slow, and two of his friends wouldn't make it. He also noticed Kate had been struggling to breathe, her weakened lung wasn't up to all this excitement, and it may have already collapsed; though Kate wouldn't say if it had. He knew she wouldn't want him to worry.

The mini hit the ramp, which scraped along the road and was soon flying through the air towards the bridge. The driver of the still chasing car decided to follow despite the protests of his colleagues. The wheels of the mini scraped the top of the metal barrier of the bridge before touching down onto tarmac again. Michael hit the brakes and spun the steering wheel, twisting the car so that the passenger side slammed into the opposite barrier.

The barrier held.

Taking quick, short breaths, Michael turned to see a car fly towards him. He barely had time to throw the mini into gear and pull out of the way of the oncoming car. Due to the fact that the ramp was moving, the following car actually jumped clean over the bridge and landed back hard on the motorway, in front of the continuing transport. The explosive coming together of the two vehicles was quite spectacular, and Michael would have said so if he had seen it, but the mini was already far from the bridge.

"I can't believe we made it." Michael said, speeding down a twisting country lane.

"We won't all make it unless we get to a hospital fast." Sally said as she slumped back into the rear seat. "Edward's unconscious and his pulse weak. Probably won't be long before I black out."

Michael could hear the weakness in her voice.

"And…" Kate struggled, gasping for breath. "It's…getting…"

"Don't talk Kate." Michael interrupted, "I can guess what you're going to say, we will make it to a hospital in time."

As Michael brought the mini rushing round a particularly sharp corner he blinked with sudden shock. Directly in front of him, just up the road, was a swirling mass of colour.

The light coming from it's centre was bright, yet strangely disconnected from his surrounding world, as if all the light was directed straight to him, nothing near the light seemed to reflect it. But he could see it, and, judging from the gasps behind, so could the girls.

"Shame you can't see this Ed." He said as the mini started to slow down.

"I ain't dead…yet…" Edward said in a hushed whisper.

"I won't be able to stop."

The mini continued into the mass of light, and vanished from the world.

All Edward could remember was a similar electricity in the air like before. The others seemed to feel it for the first time. No one witnessed the event, and when the mini was gone, the mass of swirling light was soon gone as well, leaving no trace.

DEATH COMES HARD

Part 2

"Where are we?" Michael said, looking at the alien landscape surrounding them.

The rocks and Desert like ground was deep rust-coloured red, massive mountain ranges could be seen far in the distance, on either side of them. The Land in front was hidden by a steep rise only a few hundred yards ahead. The sky was clear and pale red in colour, shot with green here and there. The land around them was beautiful yet barren.

"Forget about that, what happened to our wounds, they're gone." Sally said observing the healed skin on her legs.

"We aren't dead are we?" Mike asked.

"I don't know, but we're no longer alone" Edward said.

And he was right; they had all been so confused at what had happened that they hadn't noticed the horrid alien creatures surrounding the car.

"I don't think this is heaven," Kate confessed at the sight of the aliens.

Standing five feet tall and almost as wide, the four-armed creatures vaguely looked humanoid.

"I hope they are friendly," Sally said, fear in her voice.

"Let's find out," Michael said and wound down the window, "Hi, I don't suppose you…"

Before Michael could finish the closest alien grabbed him and pulled him out of the car through the open window. The same almost happened to Edward as an alien's four-fingered fist smashed through the window on his side and grabbed for him. Edward was quicker; he pushed away with his feet, turning to face the alien as he grabbed the car roof on the driver's side. Still moving he pulled himself out through the open window, swinging his legs up behind him as they left the car. Michael managed to duck just enough as Edward's feet passed over his head to kick the alien behind, releasing him.

Edward's movement continued as he completed his handstand on top of the car, but his pause was so brief it was unnoticeable. He carried on over and into a roll, which took him to the other side of the roof, and the moment he was in a crouch he leapt forward and over the alien's surrounding the car. The entire move took only a Matter of seconds, so the alien who had tried to grab him still had its arm through the broken window when Edward attacked.

Michael had only just started to fight himself when he heard the scream, taking a risk he glanced at the car and his fears were confirmed. Sally had been dragged out of the car as he had been, but through a broken window which left her with multiple cuts all over. Kate in the meantime was still safely inside. Michael paid the price for his risk as an alien struck him from behind and everything went black.

Edward had also heard the screams. Sally was on the other side of the car to him, but was being dragged to the back away from the fight. He kicked away his opponent and ran towards Sally and the alien, as he neared the alien threw Sally to one side and drew a strange looking weapon, but wasn't quick enough to fire it, Edward raced straight into him. They both fell to the floor and rolled down the dusty rock slope and over the edge of a hidden cliff. Sally ran to the edge and looked down in shock, some ninety feet below lay the broken, and blood covered bodies of Edward and the alien. Sally was so shocked at Edward's death that it wasn't until she heard Michael shout out that Edward's sacrifice would be meaningless if she died too, that she could take in her surroundings again.

***

Michael opened his eyes, his vision was bleary and it took him
time to focus and take in his surroundings. He was inside a cage made of solid metal bars. He guessed it hadn't been designed for humans by its sheer size and strength. Looking outside between the six-inch thick bars, he could see what could pass as a forest surrounding them. The trees were similar to those at home except for the colouring, the bark was deep red and the leaves were golden orange as if it was autumn, and they were moving past him. He shook his head to clear it, the trees weren't moving, he was! The entire cage was passing silently through the trees. He wished he could stop the buzzing in his head, but it persisted. The blow he had received had left a large lump on the back of his head and it had bled for he could feel dry blood still in his hair. He must have been out for some time. What of the others? The thought cleared his head more than any amount of shaking. He quickly scanned the inside of the cage. Kate was sleeping just to his side and seemed in no way injured. Sally was sat at the back of the cage, judged on their direction of motion. She was sat with her knees to her chest as if she was very cold and she did not move except for the shallow intakes of breath. At first Michael thought that she too was asleep, but then he noticed that her eyes were open and looking out into the distance, she seemed to be in a trance or a world of her own.

Edward was nowhere in sight and this troubled Michael a lot. Why should he be separated from the others? His train of thought was abruptly halted as a small ball of fur landed on his lap, fallen from an overhanging branch. Though Michael could not see in front or behind he figured they must be on some sort of trail. He only looked at the ball of fur to start with, it didn't look dangerous, only the size of a tennis ball and coloured bright blue, it looked somewhat out of place on this overly red world. There were no other details to be seen and after a time he figured it would be safe to touch but how wrong he was. As he touched the small fur ball he received what could only be an electric shock that sent him backward against the cage wall, into a sitting up position. Although he couldn't see it himself he knew his hair would be standing tall. The shock lasted only a spilt second, which Michael was thankful for; he was amazed that he hadn't shouted out. He gave the fur ball a queer look and blinked in surprise as two bright green eyes, the size of old ten pence pieces, looked right back at him with, it seemed, a slight menace.

"Wait a second, you didn't have eyes before?"

As if in reply the eyes turned around as if looking inside its self and the back of the eyes where covered in the same blue fur as before, leaving nothing visible but blue fur. They then carried on turning in the same direction until they faced out once more.

"Next trick", Michael said, impressed, "but why did you give me an electric shock? That really hurt a lot".

"I was defending myself". The words were not spoken they merely appeared in Michael's mind, with a definite female presence.

"You had no right to touch me!" It took Michael a few moments to gather up his thoughts and he realized the fur ball was communicating telepathically, he also decided he wasn't going to take the blame just like that.

"Who? May I ask, gave you the right to land in my lap, I had every right to move you off!"

"I didn't ask to land in your lap, it was an accident".

"Then it would be logical for you to apologize to me."

"I'm sorry I hurt you", the voice said in his mind.

"Well, now that's settled", Michael said, seeing the creature's eyes no longer held menace, "May I ask who and what you are and how you seem to know my language so well?"

"My name is unpronounceable in your tongue but my species is not, my people and I are Goeits and the answer to how I know your language is simple, we Goeits communicate telepathically and so when joining with others minds we instantly learn how that creature communicates, but I can assure you that it is not mind reading, so your memories and un-worded thoughts are safe."

"Does it work both ways?" Michael asked.

"Yes, but it will take some practice and training, but don't be mistaken, you will not become telepathic, you will only be able to communicate with others who ARE telepathic."

"Still, it would be helpful, I have a lot of questions and I don't think I will always be free to ask them out loud."

"As in your current situation?"

"Yes! If you could help us escape in some way, you could be like an extra Ace in a game of Poker to give us the upper hand."

"I do not know of this game Poker? And I do not think I will be of much help, I am too small to fight and I cannot use weapons or any other device for that Matter."

"Size does not matter and the best weapon against any enemy is knowledge! I don't know anything about this world or it's inhabitants but you do!" Michael answered and as an afterthought added, "Poker's just a game of luck and skill, I might teach you one day when we get out of here".

Kate suddenly stirred but didn't wake up.

"I think its best I hide you for now", Michael said.

"Do you not want your comrades to know about me?"

"No, not just yet, a secret is best kept when the least number of people know about it and if we keep your presence confined to just you and me it will be far harder to discover".

"You have a strange wisdom", the creature said in his mind.

"Thanks, I'll take that as a compliment, I think? Is it safe for me to touch you?"

"Yes."

"You won't electrocute me again?"

"I will not harm you again."

"Good!" Michael said, carefully picking up the small ball of fur. "By the way, how did you electrocute me?"

"I am not completely defenceless, but I do need time to recharge."

Michael placed the creature inside a pocket in what was left of his shirt.

"Recharge? How do you do that?"

"I absorb radiation of all types, a bit like eating I suppose."

"You chose when to? Eat?" Michael asked.

"Yes, if I simply continue to absorb radiation I would possibly explode, so I can block it out when I need to. I must say, this is very comfortable."

"I just hope I don't squeeze you accidentally."

"Don't worry, we're a very hardy race."

"Who are you talking to? Asked Kate, finally waking up.

"Oh, just talking to myself, trying to work things out, out loud that's all," Michael lied exceptionally well, "How long have I been out?"

"About four hours before I fell asleep, it's hard to tell without a watch." Kate replied sleepily.

"Ed's got a watch" Michael said, then suddenly realised again, "Where is Ed?"

"I'm sorry Mike, there's no easy way to say this, but not long after you were knocked out Edward fell to his death saving Sally."

Michael was lost for words. Yet for some reason it was what he had expected.

Kate continued,

"Sally was heart broken, but she didn't scream out. She just froze. She's been like that ever since."

Michael looked back at Sally; it was strange that she had only known Edward a ... Michael thought... not even a fortnight, yet she sat stony eyed and still as if she had also died. His thoughts returned to the hospital the day he found out about Kate, Death comes hard to the living, not the dying or the dead, but to the living. Sally was alive physically but had she died inside, mentally.

"Your thoughts are strong on this subject," a voice said in his head, *"in a way you are right, as I said before, you have a strange wisdom."*

***

"What is it?" said a tall athletic man who was standing in the lengthening shadow of a large rock, as the red-hot sun continued it's decent.

The man's face was aged by stress, yet he was much younger than he looked. The trials of war tended to do such things. He wore a black tight fitting jumpsuit and a jacket made from tridide hide, the toughest leather ever known and so acted much like armour. The jacket reached his feet and was as black as the void of space. Looking through deep green eyes cursed with lines, he watched his companion examine the strange object. His companion was a droid the size and shape of a basketball; fine lines almost invisible to the naked eye ran all over the surface, indicating where panels might open. The three eyes of the droid were equally spaced around the floating globe, and each was a different colour depending on function. The black metal of the droid's spherical body showed the red, blue, and green eyes up quite nicely. With each eye a constant changing shade of colour, and more than one shade being shown at a time, gave the droid an attractive look, and ability to show emotion.

"My databanks do not hold any information on this machine but it appears to be a vehicle of some kind." The droid said in a girlish voice.

"Do you detect any signs of danger?" The man's voice was the only indication left of his age. He had barely turned twenty years old.

"No danger can be detected, closest hostile life form is half a mile South by South-East."

The man gave a sigh of relief, after discovering the dead body at the base of the cliff he had been on edge. He had climbed up as quickly as he could for next to the dead alien there were drag marks. There must have been two dead bodies before he had arrived and some beast had already taken one away, possibly, the same one he had heard earlier. He stepped out of the shadow and into the fading light of the day to approach the vehicle. Comprising of four wheels, a body of a strange shape and black in colour with green strips made it look more like the many rocks, which littered the landscape. The glass was broken in the two back windows and one in the front, and the body shell seemed badly damaged. The spherical droid hovered close by as the man circled the car.

"From what I can make out of the engine at the front under the large panel, it works off a primitive liquid fuel of which I have not come into contact with before." The droid said.

"Does it still work? It looks damaged."

"The damage is only superficial and should not effect it's operating correctly."

"Then we shall make use of this thing, it will save us walking all the way."

"It also has an old radio receiving unit. I may be able to make modifications to hide us from scanning." The droid ventured as they both got inside.

"Good, we haven't much time left but this should give us the edge we need." He paused as he examined the wheel and switches in front of him.

"I believe, from my scans, that the pedal on the right sends us in motion and controls speed. The centre pedal will stop motion. The third pedal, the one on the left, will disengage the engine, allowing you to alter gear ratio, with the stick on your left; the numbers indicate gear size. Turning is accomplished using the wheel in the front of you. All other switches have no use to us at the moment."

"How do you start it up? Nothing seems to work."

"Try turning the key switch clockwise as far as it will go."

Following the droid's instructions the man finally managed to familiarise himself with the car's controls and by the time the sun had disappeared below the horizon he had the car moving quite smoothly towards his destination.

"It's damn hard when you can't see where you are going." He admitted.

"Try the switch on you right, it should turn on some lights."

"This one?" he asked pushing.

"Yes."

With the flick of the switch the land ahead became visible yet again, with the car's headlights on at full beam.

"Someone might see us now," he said, worried.

"At least you can see where you're going, I'll give you a warning when we're nearer."

"Good! I don't like spoiling surprises."

Unnoticed by both the droid and the human, a dark object moved through the shadows, somehow managing to keep up with the car.

***

Michael watched a building; looking very much like an old mediaeval castle, disappear from view as the cage he was in turned towards it. Dawn had only just started but he had been awake for some hours now, talking to the Goeit, he had named 'Blue', to find out more about this strange world. He had discovered some very disturbing information. The planet was called Autotron, which meant he and his friends were no longer on earth. Alien creatures invaded the planet almost two years ago, led by a being; the Goeits had learned, named Zaxtooum. At first the race of Goeits had tried to be friendly with these newcomers but had learned through a terrible loss that that would not be possible. A whole clan had been wiped out; they had lived where the hideous castle now stood. So the Goeits decided to disappear for they had no way with which to fight back. They were outsized, outnumbered, and the aliens had developed defences against the Goeits natural electricity. While hidden, the Goeits could simply watch and had learned a lot about their new enemy. Zaxtooum had once been a member of a race known as humans, Michael mentioned that he was of the same race but Blue had told him that only Zaxtooum's humanoid form was left of what he had once been. Zaxtooum was using the planet's natural resources, extremely high in iron, to create an army of robots and ships. He was at war with someone, yet must have been hidden for no one ever attacked. Until…. Only a day ago, a single spaceship tried to land but had been shot down before so doing. Michael had already considered, due to the technology mentioned, that he and his friends must have also travelled in time, most likely into the future. The only other information that Blue could provide was that two days before the spaceship had appeared, Zaxtooum had started to send hundreds of small ships into space. There could possibly be ten thousand ships now in orbit close by, unless he was sending small attack forces constantly at his enemy whoever that was?

Michael was still digesting the information he had discovered when the floating cage passed through the castle gates.

One glance at the walls was all he needed to know that there was no way of breaking through, being made of solid stone blocks some three feet thick and three feet high. The lengths varied between seven and ten feet. Just before the large iron doors closed, themselves being a foot thick and fifteen feet high, Michael caught a glimpse of an oil black liquid held within a diamond faced moat. It did not look very inviting. The cage continued moving until it was swallowed by a large metal lined building, lit with red tinted lights strung across the ceiling. Kate woke, just as the cage was being opened. Sally, being closest to the door was dragged roughly out, with no sign of struggling as if she was a rag doll. Michael and Kate followed, neither struggled with their alien captors, Kate knew it would be a wasted effort, Michael just simply didn't want to add to the damage he had already taken in the fight. The three of them were half led, half dragged down a broad metal corridor with more red tinted lights strung along the ceiling, strangely three meters high, twice the height of the aliens. The light gave the metal a blood red colour. After being taken down four more corridors each looking as the first, they were finally dumped into a small room some two meters square, three meters high, and obviously designed for only one prisoner. The large metal door was slammed behind them and many locks could be heard clicking into place. There was only a small air vent in the roof and a single bench, already occupied by a large human male, with wavy brown hair and deep brown eyes who sat staring directly at the newcomers.

"Who the hell are you?" he said, half rising.

"Just some unwilling guests like yourself," Michael said, "though we are not quite sure why we are here, maybe you could…"

Sally suddenly collapsed on to the floor interrupting Michael and causing the man to practically leap from the bench. He almost hit the ceiling but even for his great size he somehow managed to pick Sally from the floor and turn to lay her onto the bench within the small and crowded room. Kate was at Sally's side as quick as was possible.

"Her face is almost white," She said in a panic.

"I can't see any wounds, yet she looks like she has lost a lot of blood."

Michael considered the words of the man almost unconsciously, what had happened to all her cuts from being dragged through the broken window?

"What's wrong with her? Kate asked.

"Its Edward," Michael answered, though half his mind still pondered on her state.

"Edward? Who's Edward?" The man asked.

"He used to be her boyfriend, I knew they were in love, but not this much," Kate said.

"I take it something happened to him."

"Yes. Though I didn't see it happen myself."

"He was killed, saving Sally's life," Kate finished.

"She went into shock, I suppose you could say she died inside and now her body is catching up with her mind."

"Shock normally kills instantly, how long has she been like this?"

"A few days." Kate replied.

"I don't think there is anything we can do for her, she, and she alone holds her life in her hands. She has to decide if she wants to live or not." The man said, and knowing there was no more he could do for Sally he turned to Michael, "I don't believe we have been introduced, my name is Ice-Jock, hottest pilot alive."

"I'll believe that when I see it," Michael said shaking the man's hand, "My name is Michael Harker, this is Kate Glover and our ill friend is Sally Clarke, it's a shame you never got to meet Edward Hawk, he always wanted to fly."

"Just like his name."

"You bet."

"How did you get here?" Ice-Jock asked.

"We haven't figured that part out yet, I suppose you could say we sort of crashed, how about you?"

"I was on a mission to destroy this place, but got caught".

"Why destroy it? Michael asked, not knowing if Ice-Jock was telling all, though the man seemed to be intelligent enough not to be that stupid, any number of listening devices could be in the room, and as Ice-Jock was still alive it meant that his captors had not yet discovered everything about him. It could explain why they were all in the same cell.

"You mean you don't know?" he asked a little deviously.

"We've been out of communications for some time and haven't exactly been close to home either".

"Great! Here's me, hoping you could give me some news about the war and I end up with a couple of adventurers who don't even know there is a war!"

"A war! Who's fighting who?" Kate asked, shocked.

"You really don't know, do you?" Ice-Jock said, really quite surprised.

Michael had already discovered some information but he had kept it to himself so Kate was truly shocked.

"We're not even sure where we are," Kate added.

"Well, it looks like I have some explaining to do," Ice-Jock started.

"The human alliance discovered alien life forms a couple of hundred years ago, you should know that part at least."

"Yeah" Michael lied, getting a quizzical look from Kate, "but it might help if you explain how it all started."

"Right, Well, we now have seven different alien races joined with our alliance, now called the Alien Alliance."

"Makes sense," Michael said.

"The latest alien race to be discovered was also the largest and most hostile, even so, it was thought by many that they would join the alliance. Four years ago that belief was destroyed when the race, known as the eighth to the humans, since their true name cannot be translated, attacked and slaughtered eleven outposts by their border. No one could understand why they had attacked, though it now seems they want entire dominance over all others. Their technology is advanced but the alien alliance has a much more varied scope. It's only the fact that we are all allies that has stopped us from being destroyed so far. A year ago a scientist discovered a quick way to mass-produce fighter ships, this would give the alliance a much greater advantage and help us end the war which has already cost billions and billions of lives. Unfortunately, the eighth alien race discovered this, how, we aren't quite sure. They captured the scientist, up until a month ago no one knew what had become of him, we received a holo message by a creature called Zaxtooum and some believe that he is or used to be the scientist, though he no longer looks or acts human. In the message he demanded unconditional surrender by all or all would be destroyed."

"And you were sent here to kill him," Michael said.

"Yes."

"Alone."

"That's right, you see the defences set up here are very tight, only a small one man craft would have a chance of getting through."

"And you volunteered?"

"No, I was the only one with the skills needed to pull this off."

"I don't suppose this alliance had a back up plan?"

"None that I'm aware of."

"OK, first we get out of here and then we can help you blow this place sky high." Michael said.

"How do you propose we get out of here? I've already tried a dozen times. The vent is too small to get through, the walls are high grade steel, around five inches thick, the door is just as thick as the walls and there are inch thick steel poles on all sides locking it in place. This room is built like a safe, find an explosive powerful enough to make a hole and you would kill everyone inside." Ice-Jock said.

"We got in, didn't we?" Michael put forward.

"What's that suppose to mean?"

"There are four of us in here now, the moment they open the door…." Michael left the sentence hanging.

"Rush out, fight the aliens, they have weapons, we don't, you're crazy!"

"There aren't any other options, as you have already pointed out and besides we haven't got any thing to lose, I don't think they will let us go after the war is over."

"He's right, Ice-Jock, it's the only chance we have," Kate said.

"What about Sally?" he asked.

"We can't leave her here," Kate added.

"We'll have to carry her and hope she comes round soon,"

"If she ever comes round," Ice-Jock reminded as he sat with his back to the wall.

As if on cue the door opened but before anybody could act a tall dark figure filled the doorway. Some seven feet tall and wrapped in a long black and purple cloak which reached all the way to the floor. The face was hideous and twisted as if it had been put through great pain and had never returned to its relaxed form. The skin on the humanoid face was dark purple in colour and covered with scars and crease lines, which looked like deep cracks in very dry mud, the texture also seemed to be the same. However, it was the eyes that held everyone's gaze, they were identical to a shark's, small, deep, black and hollow looking. The face smiled.

"It appears I have caught the rest of your little group, Ice-Jock. I hope you enjoyed your little reunion, the charade was interesting but not convincing."

"What?" Ice-Jock was truly confused.

Michael was about to speak but stopped himself as he reconsidered his words. Ice-Jock hadn't come alone but he was the only one to have been caught. Which meant that someone else had the chance to complete the mission. When Zaxtooum had captured himself and his friends he must have assumed that they were the other part of Ice-Jocks team. So intent was Zaxtooum to find the others that he wrongly thought that he had. He had heard their conversation on some sort of device and had seen it as a ruse to lead him from the truth.

"I couldn't have put it better," *Blue* said in his mind.

Michael took a breath, let out a sigh and started his confession, hoping Ice-Jock would realise what was happening.

"Its no use Ice-Jock looks like he's figured it out alright."

Ice-Jock looked to Michael, surprise on his face.

Michael looked back, raised his right eyebrow, and half grinned.

"Yeah," Ice-Jock finally agreed after a time, realising what was happening, "but you didn't have to go and confirm his suspicions."

"They weren't suspicions, Ice-Jock, I am not stupid. I have very tight scanners, all in orbit, and anything, any ship, no Matter the size will easily be detected. Your ship was the only one to enter the atmosphere. There are no human settlements on this planet, so you see, it is rather quite simple, the only way these other humans, your comrades, could have gotten here was by your ship. I haven't figured out how you managed to deploy them but for now that's of no concern," Zaxtooum explained, his voice like an echo of evil itself.

"For now you will have to excuse me I have a war to win.
Don't worry I haven't finished with you yet, as it happens I have a few experiments to conduct and you're going to be my test subjects." Zaxtooum turned to leave and as he did he continued, "Just one last thing, your friend who died so heroically has just become the meal of a Dragnoor, a large ferocious beast native only to this planet. I expect he made a tasty snack for the creature. Until later...."

The door to the cell slammed shut and the locks set.

Michael turned to look at Sally, he couldn't be sure but she seemed to have paled even more.

"He knows we are planning to escape, I'm sure of it," Kate said, still at Sally's side.

"I almost had the impression that he wants us to try," Ice-Jock added.

Michael asked Blue a question in his mind, the others still unaware of his small friend. The answer put a smile on his lips. "Then let's not disappoint him."

"What's to be happy about?" Ice-Jock asked.

"We're not going to try to get out of here, we are going to get out of here. Boy is Zaxtooum going to get a hell of a shock!"

***

Zuckless pulled himself from under the car, his hands and face dirty with oil, and he started to change the wheel, now the brake cable was patched up.

"I'm glad this thing had a spare in the back, have you managed to patch the other wheels up?"

His droid companion spoke from the other side of the car, "I'm working on the last one now, I managed to get enough rubber off that other tire to do the job, but we won't be able to fix this vehicle again if you run over another patch of glass plants."

"Hey, stop trying to put the blame on me."
"You were driving."

"That's not the point, you should have given me a warning about this danger. Besides, glass plants are almost invisible to human eyes."

"If you turn the lights back on you should be able to see the reflections should there be anymore."

"Wait a minute, not that long ago you told me to turn them off because your sensors picked up a patrol of those aliens."

"Now you're trying to blame me," the Droid said, sounding like a young girl sobbing.

Zuckless thought for a moment, listening to his sad companion, for a droid she was very emotional and although Zuckless had created and programmed her she had made many modifications to herself and he felt this was not a good time to find out if she could now cry.

"Okay, I'm sorry I hurt your feelings, I guess we should both take equal blame, anyway, that's the new wheel fitted," he said finishing his work. "Are you finished your side?"

"I am now," she said, recovering her dignity a bit.

"Great, how much further to the castle?"

"I reckon on three miles, possibly four, it's hard to judge on this sort of terrain, though this forest will give us good cover yet."

"Well at least with this vehicle we've gotten well ahead of schedule."

Before the droid could give a reply there was a sudden noise not far away and a small strange looking creature ran out of the undergrowth, past Zuckless and re-entered the undergrowth on the other side of the trail.

"Little guy was spooked by something," Zuckless said, standing up, "your sensors picking up anything?"

"No, but I don't want to hang around here to find out if they're malfunctioning. I've had the feeling that something has been following us ever since we found this car," the droid said, her voice now sounding uneasy.

"You've had that feeling too," Zuckless sighed, "I thought I was imagining it, still, we better get on the move anyway, we don't want to waste all the time we have gained and since when have you had feelings?"

"Oh, for some time now, I made the changes a while back but they have only just started to work properly."

"At the rate you keep modifying yourself there won't be any of the original droid left. How am I supposed to fix you should you get damaged?"

"I won't get damaged, at least, I hope not," the Droid said, entering the car. "Actually, I'm hoping my body will be able to repair itself, I just have to do some more programming of the nanobots and…."

"OK! I get the picture", Zuckless said as he started the car, "just don't get damaged before you finish, the way you're going you'll be more human than me."

"I thought I was more human than you."

"You watch your tongue young lady, I created you and if you keep on I'll smack your hide."

"I haven't got a hide, I'm just a sphere, remember!"

"Now look, I…"Zuckless stopped and considered what was happening, "I can't believe it, I'm treating you like a kid instead of a machine, from now on we're going to drop this subject until we've completed our mission, understood?"

"Understood," the droid replied.

"Good, now lets go."

The car restarted its journey towards Zaxtooum's castle. Out of the shadows behind came a blur of motion and it followed the car, scaring another little creature deeper into the undergrowth as it went.

***

Two guards stood outside the prisoner's cell, under orders from Zaxtooum himself to keep the door shut at all times. The COM on the wall opposite started to buzz and after looking to his companion the smaller of the guards moved to answer it.

Zaxtooum's face appeared on the screen.

"I've had a change of mind," he said, "take the prisoners directly to the lab, I will arrive shortly to begin the experiments."

The guard nodded in understanding but did not speak. Switching off the COM he approached the door to the cell and explained to his companion.

The door opened.

An instant later Michael and Ice-Jock attacked, Ice-Jock taking the larger guard, though he still stood a foot taller than the opponent. Since the doors were all naturally wide due to the alien's broadness it was possible for both Michael and Ice-Jock to dive through at the same time. It's true that the aliens had the advantage in a fight, for their short height and broadness meant they had a very low centre of gravity so they were incredibly hard to knock down. The fact that they had four arms instead of two meant that they could block, parry, punch and grab all at the same time. Yet Michael still managed to defeat his opponent, kicking and punching low and practically dancing out of the way of attacks. His karate skills seemed to have become sharper; it was also a method of combat unknown to the alien. Ice-Jock relied more on pure strength than skill. He managed to wrestle his opponent to the ground and pin three of the four arms of his alien opponent. The one limb he failed to pin struck him in the face with such force that he was thrown backward into the cell.

"Need any help?" Kate asked biting her lip in sympathy of the pain Ice-Jock must have felt.

"I can take him," he said, re-finding his feet, "I can take him".

He ran back out and in mid run his punch somehow passed the alien's defensive blocks and connected nicely with the horrid creature's face. Ice-Jock then turned, holding his hand in pain, and looked at Michael who had already defeated his foe.

"You alright?" Michael asked.

"I don't know," Ice-Jock replied, "it feels broken."

"Well, hopefully it's just badly bruised, at least he won't be getting up again."

The alien Ice-Jock had hit had a bloodied and broken face and its neck was bent at an impossible angle.

"I don't believe we actually managed to pull it off." Kate said, leaving the cell.

"We? What do you mean? We?" Michael asked.

"Hey, your plan was good but I did refine it. Blue told you she couldn't control their minds just give them suggestions."

Michael's plan had been simple enough to start with. He introduced Blue to his friends, he had then told them the plan telepathically, using Blue as a go-between, since they knew the cell had listening devices. Michael had asked if Blue could control the alien's mind and get it to open the door. Blue had said that she couldn't. It was Kate that had suggested tricking the aliens instead of controlling them. The COM message had been all her idea and it had worked.

"No time to argue," Ice-Jock said, picking up the alien's weapons and handing one to Michael, "we must have triggered some sort of alarm, lets get out of here before reinforcements arrive."

"Kate, come on," Michael said, starting down the corridor to the right of the cell. They had actually gone a good ten meters before Kate realised they had left Sally behind. She was about to turn to go back when five alien warriors came round behind them and started to shoot on seeing the escaped captives.

"RUN!" Michael shouted, knowing they wouldn't stand a chance out in the open. The trio ran down the corridor until they came to a junction, shooting wildly behind them to deter their followers.

"We have to go back for Sally," Kate pleaded, as Michael and Ice-Jock returned fire.

"I know, but with those aliens down there we haven't got a chance." Michael said.

"We can't stay here long, they will have us trapped in no time." Ice-Jock said, "I'm sorry but to try and save your friend will just get us all recaptured and worse, killed!"

"The way that Zaxtooum was talking I'd rather get killed than recaptured, but that's my preference."

"Any alternatives?" Kate said.

"I have an idea," Michael said, " we can't go down there but Sally could run to us."

"In the state she's in?"

"Trust me, her pain is all in her mind, she got so close to Edward that when he died she did as well. I've been thinking about it a lot, I just have to find the right words."

"We're running out of time," Ice-Jock warned.

On that prompt Michael seemed to know vaguely what to say or rather shout, as Sally was some thirty meters away.

"Sally! I know you can hear me, Edward is dead and we all miss him but he died saving your life, he sacrificed himself for you. If you don't get a grip and accept that, his death will be meaningless, don't let Edward's death have no meaning. Stay with us and LIVE, Live for him! As long as we're alive his memory will never be lost!" Michael stopped not knowing what else to say his own words had even given him more reason to fight.

As he started shouting back at the aliens again a wonderful sight appeared. Sally came out of the cell. His joy suddenly turned to horror as he realised she was in the middle of a crossfire. He saw an alien shoot in her direction, he heard Kate shout out a warning, and suddenly Sally moved, becoming nothing more than a colourful blur coming towards him.

***

Sally had heard Michael's words and they had made sense. In fact, more sense than she would have liked, it hurt to realise that Edward had died for her, but at the same time it gave her a reason to live. Colour started to come back to her white skin and she started to breathe more easily. She suddenly sensed an urgency to move, taking a quick look at her surroundings she rose from the hard bench on which she had lay and stood up on her shaking legs. A moment later she stepped out into the corridor. Bright flashes of light passed her in both directions, she had stepped right into a firefight with no protection. She heard Kate shout a warning and turned to see an alien aim for her and shoot. Everything slowed down. Sounds became meaningless and distant, the colourful laser blasts floated through the air with grace and purpose. Sally watched a laser bolt of red-hot intensity fly towards her, she knew she had to get out of the way or be killed, and she would not let Edward's death have no meaning.

She moved.

It was like being in a dream when everything is in slow motion and the faster you try to run from the horror that chases you, the slower you actually seem to go. But Sally wasn't dreaming and she did run fast, very fast. She could see everything so clearly yet movement, other than her own was horribly slow. The red laser bolt which had been fired at her was suddenly left far behind and she dodged quickly to the side to stop herself running through another red beam actually moving away from her, it's proper target being Michael. She tackled him down to the ground and rolled with him around the corner for cover. Play mode was suddenly switched back on.

"What hit me?" Michael said, his back against the floor. Looking up he answered his own question, "Sally?"

"Sorry I had to take you down like that, but you would have been killed if I hadn't," she said, her voice shaking after what she had experienced.

"Would you mind if I got up?" He asked.

"Oh, sorry," Sally said and shakily got off Michael who was helped up by Kate.

"What just happened back there?" Ice-Jock said, "How did you move so fast?"

"I don't know," Sally answered truthfully.

Ice-Jock was about to put another question forward when he was suddenly hit on his left shoulder by a laser blast. He shouted out in pain as he instinctively used the blast's momentum to twist his body back behind the corner.

"How bad is it?" Michael asked retrieving his blaster from the floor.

"Went through the bone," Ice-Jock said gritting his teeth, "but it seems pretty clean, I'll be OK when the pains' died down a bit."

Kate picked up Ice-Jock's fallen blaster, which had skidded to her feet.

"Which way do we go?" Michael asked, wanting to get as far away from where he presently was as soon as possible.

Kate lifted the weapon and found it quite comfortable, even natural.

"Either way will do for now," Ice-Jock answered.

"I don't suppose you know your way around then."

"Only vaguely."

Kate fired the weapon.

Of the five guards that had started the shoot-out, one had been killed by Ice-Jock. Kate fired four times.

Silence.

Michael stood looking towards the enemy. His mouth hung open. Ice-Jock, confused by the silence edged his way from the cover of the wall to look down the corridor. The sight that greeted his eyes was impressive; a single shot to the head had killed each of the remaining four alien guards. He looked to Kate, still holding the blaster,

"You should have told us you were a crack shot,"

Michael closed his mouth as he considered his next words,

"Kate has never fired a gun before," he said, "in fact, she's never held a gun before."

"Don't ask me how, but it felt so...." She hunted for the right word.

"Natural." Sally finished for her, "I felt the same when I ran, as if it was something I'd done many times before, which it is, but not the way I ran past those blaster shots."

"You guys holding something back that I should know about?" Ice-Jock said looking at them in awe.

"It seems we've been altered somehow." Michael guessed.

"By Zaxtooum?" Ice-Jock asked, shocked.

"No." Michael said, "by something else entirely, probably the same something which brought us here."

"And healed our wounds." Kate finished.

"Wait a minute, didn't you say you crashed?"

"We don't have time to talk about this right now." Sally said.

Michael agreed, "Ice-Jock, you lead the way, once your task is completed and we are all out of here, then we can try and explain what's happened."

Ice-Jock went to go down his chosen corridor when he stopped and looked back at Michael, "What do you mean, try to explain?"

"We haven't figured it out for ourselves yet," Michael admitted.

***

Commander Laytoo took the report from a subordinate. The news was grim. As he made his way to Zaxtooum's side he wondered how the captives had managed to escape their cell. He also knew that head's would roll for this incompetence and hoped his wouldn't be one of them. Zaxtooum hated bad news. He reached Zaxtooum and handed the report over, his bright yellow skin paled as he waited for the reaction to follow. He was of a different alien species to the four-armed thugs who provided all the muscle for Zaxtooum's army, even though they had little intelligence. In fact, Commander Laytoo didn't even think they should be classed as sentient. In contrast Laytoo's species were highly intelligent and though their bodies were small and their limbs long and thin, they still possessed small skill in armed combat. Commander

Laytoo also stood a good foot taller than Zaxtooum, even though he was short for his race. Zaxtooum took the report and considered its meaning and the effect it could have on his plan. Commander Laytoo found the cold silence and stillness of his master even worse than the anger he had seen on countless occasions. He almost leapt out of his skin when Zaxtooum spoke.

"Both guards are dead and it is believed one of them opened the cell door." It was a statement rather than a question, his voice as cold as ice.

"Yes, Master." Commander Laytoo blundered, "and a squad of five troops were also killed, they had reacted to the silent alarm."

"There's no need to repeat what's in the report." Zaxtooum said, his temper rising at the incompetence of the alien's around him. He had once been human and knew how determined humans could get but he wasn't human anymore. He was a new entity, transformed by his own experiments; he was above them all! He had planned to create more like himself but so far all his attempts at repeating the experiment had failed and now his test subjects were on the loose and could jeopardise everything.

"Triple security at all major control rooms, ready my elite guard and double all patrol squads. I want those humans, try and keep at least one of them alive. Don't fail me Commander or you will become a new test subject, understand?"

"Yes, Master," Commander Laytoo shakily answered.

"And step up production of the Drones, I'm bringing forward the scheduled invasion, we will now attack in four hours."

"Yes, Master," Commander Laytoo said again and watched as Zaxtooum left the control room, before giving out orders of his own. He would not fail, he could not fail.

***

Laser blasts exploded all around the escaped captives as they struggled to find cover.

"We are never going to get to the control tower like this," Michael said, wildly shooting back at the patrol they had encountered. A group of ten aliens were blocking the corridor, all with tough body armour and personal shields, so even Kate's deadly shots did no damage.

"We're going to be trapped before long," Ice-Jock said, wishing he could pass through the metal wall he was pressed against.

"We're all likely to be dead before then," Michael disagreed.

"These weapons are useless against that shielded armour," Kate said.

"There must be some sort of weak point," Michael hoped.

Sally watched their attackers continue to shoot at them and ... "I've got an idea", she said.

"I'm all ears," Ice-Jock said.

"Kate, shoot the weapons, try and hit the barrels square on."

Michael smiled, understanding, as Kate fired at her targets. She was sharp, fast and above all on target every time. Each of the alien's laser guns exploded as a laser went down the barrels in the wrong direction. It needs to be pointed out here that Laser guns don't shoot lasers; rather, they shoot small amounts of high-energy plasmatic gas so the blasts don't travel at the speed of light. It also means that the laser gun has to have storage of this special plasmatic gas to be charged and fired in small quantities. The gun's containers normally hold around fifty shots. Should these all go off at once, in ten laser guns, the resulting explosion is nothing but dramatic.

***

Zuckless stopped the vehicle just inside the forest boundary and looked ahead to the solid structure built a mere half-mile away from him. It was huge. Possibly covering more than four miles square. There was no doubt in his mind that it was only the very tip of the iceberg. His mission was to destroy the central control room and at least do enough damage to stop its production of war droids and vessels. Intelligence had discovered the place with massive space telescopes and had worked out its place in Zaxtooum's plans as being his main production and storage facility for his armies. Knowing that Zaxtooum spent most of his time there added that extra incentive to destroy the place, hoping to destroy Zaxtooum at the same time. Pulling a hand screen out of his pocket he studied the aerial plan created by the space telescopes, two key points had been marked in red, and these were the most important areas. Close to the centre was a main control tower, some half mile high. On the far side, infrared and other devices had indicated the power source, a reactor core some hundred meters square. When given the mission he had not realised the scale of the targets. Now he felt he was looking at an impenetrable citadel. This wasn't going to be as easy as he had first thought.

"You know, all that extra time we have gained is not going to help us much," his Droid companion said.

Zuckless took a moment to recompose himself and sighed,

"We have a job to do, so lets do it. That place was designed to defend against an army or heavy assault. I'm sure there's a gap in security for a single person to get in. We'll have to leave the vehicle here though, the moment we leave the shielding effect of the trees the sensors are sure to pick it up,"

"Maybe I should stay here as well?"

"Why?"

"Backup, besides you're going to need some sort of escape plan."

"I've a feeling this was a one way mission, but you're probably right."

Zuckless checked out his equipment before leaving the car,

"I'm going to try and scale that tower, near the wall," he said, pointing to one of the many towers surrounding the citadel's perimeter.

"Hoping there's a computer station in there?" the Droid guessed.

"Yeah, I'll have to pull some sort of schematic of the place, won't be much good if I get lost in there. Wish me luck." he finished and broke into a quick jog that would carry him over the rough open terrain.

"Just come back alive," she whispered knowing Zuckless was already too far away to have heard.

***

The dust and smoke began to settle and the tremors died down. The corridor had been bent and twisted where the ten aliens had once existed, now only a few scant remains of them were left.

"Now THAT was impressive." Michael said as he picked himself up off the floor.

"They must have felt that half way through the building," Ice-Jock stated, also getting up off the floor where the blast had knocked him down.

"You know, if we keep running into patrols like that we're never going to make it to the main control room," Kate said.

"Do we have to go there? Surely we could use another terminal to do the damage you intend," Sally said as she tucked her blonde hair behind her left ear.

"We'll still be running into patrols whichever option we take," Ice-Jock said.

"Then lets not use the corridors," Michael said.

"What else can we use?" Kate asked.

"The air vents, it would seem we just disappeared. I'm sure they have already concentrated all security at the main control centre, so, the other terminals wouldn't be any where near as protected."

"Then we shall try this new plan," Ice-Jock said hoisting his laser gun, "lead the way."

Michael quickly backtracked down the corridor they had come from until he came to an air-vent covered with a grid. Prising it open with the butt of a laser gun he climbed inside the half-meter square opening.

"I reckon that all the control rooms are at the top of towers, so, if we can find a shaft going up it should take us straight to some computer terminals," he said dragging himself deeper into the air-vent.

"Do you think this will be safer than the corridors?" Kate asked following Ice-Jock into the vent.

"I hope so," Ice-Jock said.

Sally was the last to enter and left the task of closing the grid. Just as she got it back into place she heard movement from outside in the corridor. She peered out to see Zaxtooum; he turned the corner and entered the corridor they had just exited. It was the first time she had seen the horrid creature but her friend's brief description was enough to recognise him. Following Zaxtooum were six guards, each different in size, shape and colour but none resembled the four-armed aliens she had already encountered. Though all were vaguely humanoid in size and shape each had a significant difference. There was a sleek, slim, jade skinned humanoid with bright purple eyes, jet black hair down to her waist and moved with a wet fluid motion almost cat like. She was the most humanoid and the only attractive one. Another two were also female or what you could vaguely pass as female. One with sharp dagger like teeth, red skin and completely devoid of hair with an extra appendage on her back and front. The other was blue skinned, very muscular and in fact the largest of the creatures, covered in multiple joints on the arms, legs and double waist. Sally reckoned she could put her body into almost any twisted position naturally. With four eyes, no nose or ears, this blue skinned woman was exceptionally ugly. The men's alterations were just as vast if not more so. One had yellow skin that was covered in a horrid puke green like goo, four arms and four legs and virtually no face to speak of. The last two had horribly contrasting skin colours but were almost the same shape and size, being about five feet tall but also five feet wide, they had two arms wider and longer than Sally's entire body yet legs only a foot long. One was pea green and the other bright pink. Neither Zaxtooum nor the guards appeared to carry any weapons Sally guessed they didn't need any.

She was about to move when Zaxtooum spoke.

"These humans are really starting to annoy me," he said, on seeing the aftermath of the explosion further down the corridor.

"They must be close by, I want each of you to use the new talents that I have given you and find them before they do some real damage."

The creatures started their search splitting up, and Sally realised that they weren't individual alien species but scientific creations. She was certain that at least some of the subjects had not been willing. How many rejects had been destroyed in his experiments? Experiments, Ice-Jock had explained to her, of which some Zaxtooum had performed on himself.

Suddenly realising she might be found; she quickly edged her way further into the vent to catch up with the others. She just hoped she would soon reach a junction so she could turn around. She had to get in the vent backwards so she could close the grill.

***

An unknown figure wrapped in a night black cloak stepped out of the shadows and looked at the massive wall which towered above it. A two-meter wide moat lay between it and the grey stonewall. The moat was diamond faced and came right up to the wall, whatever the purple/black fluid was, which was held in the diamond walls, actually seemed quite harmless. However, the cloaked figure knew that looks could be deceiving, and yet it didn't plan to find out either. After staring at the wall for some time it turned and walked away, but it did not intend to leave. Instead it turned back and moved swiftly towards the wall, jumping the moat, and smacking the grey stone with a thud. Either gravity was not aware of the cloaked figure or the cloaked figure had somehow managed to find something to hold onto. It soon became clear that the latter was the case as the figure started to scale the smooth surface.

***

Michael pulled himself up the last few feet and entered another vent at the very top of the vertical shaft. They had found the shaft not long after entering the air vents. In fact Michael had actually fallen down it but managed to twist his body and jam himself in before he fell too far. The shaft was so deep that the bottom was well out of sight but the top was only a hundred feet away. Michael had also found out that his old climbing skills had somehow managed to increase ten fold. He had found it so easy to climb up the half-meter square shaft that he ended up being turned into a human lift, carrying his friends, one by one, up the shaft. He now helped Sally over the edge then finally sat down on the edge to catch his breath.

"I know I like climbing but that's the last time I act as a living lift, from now on just one passenger, me!"

"We would never have climbed up here without your help," Kate said, lying next to Sally in the cramped ventilation shaft.

"She's right," Ice-Jock said from further up.

"So was I right, is there a control room up here," Michael asked, while he had been ferrying the girls up. Ice-Jock had been scouting ahead.

"There is, and only four guards and two computer controllers are in the room. I just hope we can lock ourselves in and use those terminals to break into the main computer,"

"As long as they're connected I should be able to pull anything off. I might be good at martial arts but computing has always been my main passion, just show me a keyboard." Michael said.

"So, how do we take out the present occupants of the room?" Sally asked.

"As quickly and as quietly as we can," Michael said.

"Do we have a plan better than that?" Kate asked.

"Nope," Michael said, "lets just improvise."

"I just hope none of those creatures Sally described find us. They sounded pretty nasty," Ice-Jock said as he led the way to the computer room.

***

Zuckless reached the outside wall and moat without incident and just hoped he wasn't walking into a trap. He looked at the moat; the purple/black liquid lay still and he knew what it was. NOA, Nano Organic Acid. A new solution created by the scientists many years ago as a weapon to use in the war, an acid so potent that it could dissolve anything but diamond in seconds. Far more powerful than pure sulphuric acid, but it was too expensive to make and the process too dangerous so it was dropped from the weapon scheme. He looked up at the towering wall, which stood on the opposite side of the moat. It didn't look quite as big from the car but close up he could barely see the top. Movement caught his eye, half way up the wall something was climbing. It had no features but wore a flowing black cloak. Yet, he felt that it was the same thing that had been following him ever since finding the car. At some stage it had obviously managed to get well in front of him. Hoping the creature was on his side he proceeded to pull a small grappling hook and fine cord from his pockets. Aiming high up towards the top of the wall he fired the hook and was glad to see that it had both caught and was long enough. The creature didn't seem to notice the event or seemed not to care that Zuckless was about to follow it up. Attaching the cord to a small pulley at his belt he put on some gloves and swung across the moat. Placing both feet on the wall, keeping them far from the acid as he could. Activating the small belt pulley he slowly walked his way up the wall, holding the cord with both hands. He'd soon catch the unknown being up and hoped again that they were on the same side.

***

Kate eased her way passed Ice-Jock within the cramped air vent and drew her gun. She hadn't been surprised that she had been chosen to rid the room of all hostiles but she would have preferred some other plan. She peered through the grill and got a fix on her targets. She would take the armed guards first and then the computer controllers. She recognised the four-armed aliens but the controllers were of a different species of alien, she hadn't seen these before. Standing almost nine feet tall and yellow skinned with wiry arms and legs she couldn't make out whether they were good fighters or not. Before acting she took in the rest of the room's contents, looking for possible cover and hidden enemies. The room had two doors, one in each wall either side of the grate. Directly opposite was a massive black window and looked as if it could be used as a large computer screen. Through it she could see the forest about half a mile away. The room also contained two large computer terminals; these seemed to be the room's only contents besides the aliens. Kate took a deep breath and let it out slowly, no more time for delays this was it.

The grate to the air vent flew open.

Kate dropped to the ground, her finger dancing on the laser gun's trigger. The guards took a moment too long to act and all lay dead on the floor. The other aliens seemed much quicker thinking. One dived for cover, but in vain. The other managed to hit some sort of alarm and sirens began to sound. Kate landed onto the floor and took cover keeping her aim on one of the doors. Michael was soon by her side and Ice-Jock and Sally took guard over the other entrance.

"Not as clean as I had hoped," Michael said.

"Six targets in two heartbeats isn't easy", Kate shouted over the noise, "just get to work on those computers. The quicker you're finished the quicker we can get out of here," Kate continued annoyed at Michael's remark.

Taking a seat at one of the terminals Michael quickly got to grips with the strange keyboard layout, far quicker than he thought he could. Within moments the alarms stopped sounding. Michael also stopped,

"That wasn't me," he said and then continued with the task in hand.

"Get ready, the attack could come at any moment," Ice-Jock said.

Kate brought the laser gun sight to her eye, her body half hidden by the terminal Michael was working at.

"I don't like this," Sally said, "now its too quiet."

"Yes! I'm in." Michael shrieked.

As was the enemy as both doors swung open. Guards charged in both entrances, not suspecting such strong resistance as alien bodies started to pile up on the floor.

"There's too many, we're never going to get out of this one," Sally said, fighting in vain.

"I'm almost finished, just hold them off a little longer," Michael said.

Suddenly he saw a reflection in the screen he was studying. They hadn't covered their own entrance, the vent shaft was still wide open and now someone else was using it. He jumped to the side, pulling Kate down with him as green flames engulfed the computer terminal. Looking up he could see the jade green female Sally had described to them. Attractive and very deadly! The woman's crimson eyes looked down at him but before she could breathe her acidic fire again Sally attacked. Michael had but a moment to act.

"Kate, here's my gun, use both and shoot like a crazed man-er-woman, I'm going to put the other terminal to use, I'm almost finished."

Before Kate could answer Michael was gone. She started shooting two weapons, the alien guards held back more.

***

Sally saw the green flame out of the corner of her eye and knew it was trouble.

"Ice-Jock, catch!" she shouted and then tossed her laser gun as she turned and struck the jade woman. She hit out twice before her opponent could react. Both women appeared masters at unarmed combat and as they fought Sally could see another misfit enter the room by the air vent. The others were too big to enter that way, Sally guessed. Most probably they were just outside the room with only the other aliens in their way. The four-armed woman finally jumped out of the air vent and attacked Michael who was still working at the terminal.

"I'm not finished yet!" Sally heard Michael cry as he began to defend himself against the creature.

Sally suddenly realised her opponent had forced her into the open; an easy target for the alien's still coming in. Kicking away she managed to flip through the air and land, with her back to the wall and some two meters from the woman. She was in temporary cover from the guards, but not out of the way of the woman's green fiery breath. She screamed as the flames reached out towards her and then everything went black. It took her a few heartbeats to realise she had neither passed out nor been hit by the fire. Something or someone in a deep black cloak had appeared between her and the fire, no, not appeared, landed. She looked up to see the smashed glass that had failed to stop this new creature's entrance. She looked on as the cloaked figure advanced on the jade woman, picked her up by the waist and throw her into the far wall, knocking her out cold. The shooting seemed to stop for a moment as everyone took in this new development. The alien's, deciding the cloaked creature was just another enemy to kill, started shooting once more. Yet any shots that were on target didn't appear to harm the creature, only damage its cloak. Sally, still crouched on the ground, watched as the figure turned and approached her. She accepted the human hand, which appeared out of the cloak to help her up, but still could not see anything within the darkness of the hood.

"Who are you?" She said.

There was no answer. The creature, still holding Sally's arm, simply threw her to the other side of the room. The four-armed, red skinned woman had Michael's arms pinned and was strangling him with her middle arm. Sally's trajectory took her right towards the creature's head. She saw the situation and clothe-lined the creature. All three hit the ground, only two stood up.

"Thanks Sal," Michael said, holding his neck, "I thought I was a gonna' just then."

"Don't thank me, it was that guy in the cape that chucked me over here."

Michael looked in the indicated direction and watched as the black cloaked figure moved to the door, which Ice-Jock was trying to cover, and casually slammed it shut, catching one unfortunate alien's arm which fell to the floor, still clutching a laser gun.

"That guy's strong," Michael stated.

"I know," Sally said, but was so lost in thought she didn't hear Michael's next remark.

"I've got a job to finish, you better help Kate."

Instead Sally just stood for a moment, before moving slowly towards the cloaked man, who still held the door shut with his brute strength alone. Ice-Jock, with no targets now to shoot at, turned just in time to see another dark cloaked figure smash through the still partially complete window, hitting the door, knocking it closed.

"Zuckless! You made it," he said, happy to see his partner and long time friend.

"No prob...." Zuckless replied as he got knocked back outside the room as the door swung back open. Kate fired four times but the lasers, all on target, didn't even scratch the square like creature, which stood in the doorway. The bright pink scales appeared to be the perfect armour. The creature stomped into the room causing small tremors with every step. Another, bright green creature followed it in.

"Great, all we're missing now is one humongous ugly looking female and a faceless male with eight limbs. But hey, I'm finished, let's leave before they arrive." Michael said, rising from the terminal block.

"Any ideas how we manage that?" Kate asked, backing away from the oncoming creatures, which thankfully, were exceptionally slow moving.

"Will someone give me a hand," the voice came from outside and Ice-Jock was soon by the window helping his friend.

"Who's he?" Michael said.

"Zuckless, my partner, we split up to double our chances of success."

"I've got a rope we can use to get down."

"That's not a rope, it's as thin as a piece of cotton." Kate remarked.

"Actually, it's high tensile cord which can hold over ten thousand Kilo Newtons with ease."

"Could we stop all this talking and get the hell out of here, I know the alien's have stopped shooting but those two large freaks are getting closer and they look like they could do a hell of a lot of damage." Michael said, backing further away.

***

Sally stood behind the cloaked man with hope and anticipation. What if she was wrong? No! She wasn't, she knew she wasn't.

"Edward?" she asked in almost a whisper, "is that you?"

The cloaked figure turned to look at Sally,

"What took you so long to figure it out?" he asked.

Sally was filled with sudden joy and pulled back the hood to look upon Edward's face, which smiled back.

Throwing her arms around him, she started kissing him on the face, the mouth, the cheeks, the eyes, just smothering him with kiss after kiss.

"Sal", he tried to say as she kissed him on the mouth, "Sal, 'm trying to hold a door shut."

She ignored his plea and Edward just gave up, "What the hell", he said, and wrapped his strong arms around Sally and kissed her back. He had been so concerned about her over the last few days that he was just as glad to finally hold her again as she was he.

Without Edward now holding the door nothing stopped the aliens from pushing it open and forcing their way into the room. Though only one actually made it, as Edward kicked it shut again, Sally still in his arms, with their mouths pressed together in passion. The one that had managed to get in died in an instant after Kate turned to see it. Though seeing Edward and Sally in each other's arms had almost caused her to miss for the first time.

"Edward! Good to see you still alive, but could we finish the reunion after we've all escaped," Michael said. He had also turned to see how the door had slammed again.

"OK, it's set up," Zuckless said, "we just slide down this and we're home free."

"What with?" that cords too fine, it will cut our hands off half way down." Michael said.

"This is a survival belt and it comes with three slip slide holds."

"There's six of us," Kate said.

"And, the stompy twins have almost reached us," Michael added.

"Two to a hold, no problem."

"We will go first," Ice-Jock said, "show you how it's done."

"We haven't got time for demo's, just go," Michael said.

Zuckless and Ice-Jock clipped onto the cord and jumped through the window. Michael was impressed, the thin cord held. A hand smashed through the door that Edward was holding shut, with one foot.

"We're out of time," Michael said, seeing the blue hand disappear back through the hole, "Miss Ugly has arrived."

"Get going," Edward insisted, "I'll hold them back."

"You better not die on us again," Michael said and grabbed Kate around the waist clipped the hold onto the cord and jumped through the window before she could protest.

"OK, we're up," Sally said, but before she or Edward could reach the cord the stompy twins finally reached the terminal that Zuckless had used as an anchor point. With one massive pink fist the terminal block was destroyed. The cord broke free and was pulled towards the window where it caught on a piece of glass. Edward grabbed the cord before it could break free again and wrapped it around his hand.

"Sally, go!" he said, holding the cord taught.

"I'm not leaving you again," she refused.

"Sally," he said, his voice much softer, "trust me, I'm not going to die up here."

Edward looked once to the door, which had been pounded out of shape by the creature on the other side so much that it wouldn't open properly, and once to the stompy twins who continued their advance.

"Sally, please, we haven't got time to argue about this."

"I don't want to lose you again," she said, tears starting to form in her eyes.

"You won't, I promise, now go."

With great reluctance Sally clipped the hold onto the cord and jumped through the window. The cord dug deep into Edward's hand but he refused to let go, even when he heard the door fall to the ground and see a blue hand grab his arm in a vice like grip. Not until Sally had made it to the ground did he turn to look at the hideous female creature standing over him? All joints and muscle, the creature's body was horribly deformed. He released the cord and with the same hand punched up at his attacker, striking nicely to the head. The creature's head fell back at an impossible angle and after a time righted itself. Before Edward could attack again the creature dove on top of him sending him to the ground. Edward suddenly felt a pain in his ribs as the blue skinned woman wrapped her powerful arms around his middle like two large ropes. She would squeeze him to death and appeared to be succeeding. Edward felt a rib snap as he gathered his strength to break free. Strength he had never even dreamed of having. He knew he had changed.
He remembered the fall he had taken and the massive creature, he later learned to be called a Dragnoor, dragging his broken body away. All he

could think about was Sally and his friends. As he was dragged along the canyon floor he had felt a strange sensation pass through his body as his bones began to change. He felt that the life or death situation he was in had somehow speeded up his body's alteration. Before long his bones had healed and hardened and he felt great strength serge within him.

He had escaped the Dragnoor to discover the creature was more intelligent than it looked, and was in fact more intelligent than his own species. He had learned a lot during that first day including the extent of his own strength, which he now called on.

With his arms pinned to his sides, he brought his knees to his chin and then flexed every muscle in his body. His reward was a scream of pain from his opponent as he ripped off her arms to free himself. Standing, he chucked the arms away from him and looked down at the blue skinned woman, she had passed out. He held his side where he now felt three broken ribs and remembered, too late, about the other two creatures still in the room as a bright pink hand, the size of a football, grabbed his right arm and squeezed. Immediately Edward realised why they were so slow, they were solid and had such a mass that not even with his strength could he pull away. The creatures seemed rooted to the ground. He cried out in pain as the blood vessels, skin, bone and other tissue in his arm were crushed. Blood shot from his arm where the pressure was too great and the creature continued to squeeze. He had to think fast or the other bright green twin would soon have him in his clutches to.

Edward had another power; he had discovered it only moments ago when he had to protect Sally from the jade woman's green acidic flame, the power to project a skin-tight field of invincibility, making him virtually indestructible for a few moments. He used that power now as he smashed his free hand into the computer terminal and grabbed the power cables. High Voltage electricity of an uncountable value surged over his skin finding no way past his invisible shield. The inhuman creature crushing his arm had no such protection and the electricity passed through the creature like lightning through a tree to earth, the terminal exploded with a force so great that it sent the creature reeling backwards. Edward was free from his opponent and the explosion had thrown him further away from the green coloured twin. He was still badly injured, though not from the explosion, and looking closer to his arm he could see the full extent of the damage and found himself looking away from the gruesome sight in shock. He removed his burnt cloak and

used it to wrap up his bloody arm.
Another deformed creature entered the room.
Edward looked at it, four arms, four legs and not even a hint of a face just a featureless globe sat on top of the neck. The vile yellow/green coloured creature ran at him with great speed determined to destroy him.

"I've had enough," Edward said, mainly to himself and dived out of the window before the creature could close the gap.

***

The ride down was fast and exhilarating but Sally was not in the mood to enjoy it. She reached the bottom of the slide and the moment her feet touched the ground the cord went suddenly slack. Turning, she could just make out the cord fall away from the window, but from the angle she was at now she couldn't see Edward. For a moment it was quiet, too quiet and then suddenly there was a shout of pain followed by a massive explosion, which took out what was left of the large window. Sally feared the worst and her heart skipped a beat when she saw Edward dive out of the building.

"Oh No! If he lands in that moat he'll be killed for sure," Zuckless said, but he couldn't think of any way to save Edward. The group was some seventy feet away from the moat, due to the angle of the slide he had created and there wasn't anything to hand to use to catch him even if they had been close enough. Everyone was stunned by Zuckless's words and it was too late too quickly, Edward landed in the moat and disappeared from view.

"NO!" Sally shouted and was off like a shot, literally, running to the moat as fast as she could. So fast that she reached the edge long before Kate's mind linked with hers.

"He isn't dead; I can still feel his mind." The projected thought stunned both Sally and Kate.

Blue joined in, *"You're as telepathic as I am, in fact, stronger; I sensed it earlier in the cell."*

"I'm telepathic?" Kate said, aloud in shock.

"You're telepathic?" Zuckless asked.

"Let's not go that way with the conversation yet," Michael said, confused, "We have to get as far away from here as we can before my alterations to that control computer take full effect. Is Edward still alive?"

"Yes," Kate answered unsure how she knew exactly.

"Then tell him to get a move on."

"He said he's going to need some clothes, his have been eaten by the acid."

"The acid did not harm him?" Zuckless asked.

"No," Kate said as she spied the jacket Zuckless wore, "May I borrow your coat?"

"I can't believe it," Michael said, as Zuckless handed Kate his beloved tridide leather jacket, who in turn passed it to Sally, who was moving so fast it was as if the jacket just disappeared, "We're the only humans on this entire planet, next to a massive citadel which is about to go supernova, I reversed the control rods in the fission generator, if anyone wants to know. It should blow in another ten minutes or so, and Edward is worried about his nudity!"

"Well it is cold out here," Kate said, defending Edward, although she wouldn't mind seeing him naked.

"It's cold," Michael said, "what do you mean its cold? Edward's just survived a highly concentrated and extremely strong acid bath, I don't think the cold will bother him much."

"Here he comes now," Ice-Jock said, as Sally, now moving at an ordinary running pace, appeared with Edward by her side. They were soon all together again.

"Shouldn't we all be on the move?" Edward asked, as he stopped next to his friends, "it shouldn't be long before they send a load of troops out to get us."

"We were waiting for you." Michael said and his voice softened, "and it's good to have you back with us."

"That it is, I never dreamed I'd see you again," Sally said, her arm around him.

"I see my jacket fits." Zuckless noticed, "and I have to know, were you the one following me?"

"Yes, I was and that Mini will give us a good edge in getting away. As for the jacket, it's a bit tight but I'm definitely going to have to get one of my own."

"I know a good dealer."

"You know, you look completely different without glasses." Kate observed, "more attractive."

"Yeah he is isn't he." Sally added, "can you see okay without them?"

"Better than ever."

"Great, now we have the reunion out of the way could we get the hell out of here, that explosions going to cover a good two to three square miles." Michael paused, "Kate, what do you mean, more attractive?"

"I never thought glasses suited Edward, but don't worry. Its you I love." Kate said before kissing Michael.

Their kiss broke,

"Hope we get some privacy later." Michael said and added telepathically, *"Blue, better tell your people to move out."*

"Already done," Blue said in his mind.

They ran over the open dirt covered ground, the blood red sun high in the sky, and soon reached the black mini. After some quick introductions to the droid they all managed to squeeze inside. Sally had to sit on Edward's lap, with Kate and Zuckless also packed in the back with them, Ice-jock being the largest got to go in front with the droid, and of course Michael was in the driving seat.

"Now, I'll show you just how to drive this little beauty properly." He said.

"Just don't hit anymore space/time rifts, don't want to jump another thousand odd years into the future," Edward said.

Michael had the car started and was zipping through the trees in no time.

"You're all from the past," Ice -Jock said, "so that's how you got on the planet without a ship."

"And we all entered that rift injured. I've a feeling whatever healed us took the healing too far and ended up improving us, giving us these powers," Edward added.

"Not just the injuries," Michael said, "old skills have been impressively increased as well."

"Concentrate on driving Mikey," Kate nagged.

"Yes mam'," he joked.

"How did you figure all this out?" Ice-Jock asked.

"It wasn't me, it was the Dragnoor which carried me off for lunch who explained it."

"Wait a minute, it didn't eat you?" Kate said.

"Dragnoors are intelligent?" Zuckless said.

"Wow! Slow down, I see this is going to take some explaining."

The ground shook violently as an unnatural earthquake began. The car became almost uncontrollable but Michael continued his suicidal pace through the trees.

"What's happening?" Kate asked Michael.

"The fission generator is subterranean, that was just a small tremor set up by escaping gas. I guess it's getting pretty hot down there and the pressure is getting too great to hold. Maybe a few miles won't be enough after all!"

"How long?" Zuckless asked.

"About four minutes, why?"

"Our ship will be a quicker way out of here."

"How far away is it?" Kate asked.

"Twenty, Twenty five miles, it was as close as I could get."

"We aren't going to get that far," Michael said.

"Just get us to a clearing, a large clearing, the ship will come to us."

"Someone else on board?"

"No, but I do have a homing beacon, the computer's not intelligent but it can get here and fast."

"Just as long as it's fast, that's all that counts."

"We're coming up to a clearing on your right," Sally said, looking through the trees.

"It'll do," Zuckless said as he pressed a few buttons on a wrist strap.

Michael reached the clearing and stopped the car, "Two minutes to an all over tan."

The ground started shaking again.

"Though I could be wrong," he added.

"I hope not," Sally said.

"Here she comes!" Zuckless shouted and pointed to a dark speck in the sky, which quickly grew larger.

Edward and Michael watched in awe. There was not a single straight line visible upon the craft, which was very sleek and feminine. The ship just seemed to flow perfectly from all angles. There were two small domed gun turrets on either side and the cockpit was a massive jet-black dome on the front. The overall shape and shell of the spaceship was similar to an elongated ladybird and had a split tail. She had pushed back wings like a jet plane, with claw shaped ends and a fan like frill around the front, which didn't meet in the middle but stopped either side of the cockpit. To finish the impressive craft, it was coloured electric blue. They watched small, black landing legs lower as the ship settled on the ground facing them.

"So, what do you think," Ice-Jock said, noticing the eye's which admired his baby.

"That is a beautiful lady," Michael said.

"You know, I'd love to sit and look at that ship all day," Edward said, "But, in less than a minute we'll all be dead," He looked at Sally, "if we don't get the hell out of here that is."

"I hear you," Zuckless said and pressed a few more buttons on his wrist strap. The ship, some twenty meters wide and fifty meters long, lowered a large cargo ramp under its belly.

"Drive on up," Ice-Jock said, opening the passenger side door.

Michael put his foot down and the car skidded inside. Moments before the car stopped inside the hold, Ice-Jock had jumped out and was running for the cockpit, while Zuckless proceeded in closing the cargo ramp. A bright flash managed to make itself visible before the ramp finally closed.

"The generator just blew," Michael said, Matter of fact.

"We aren't going to make it", Kate realised.

"Yes we are," Edward said.

There was a sudden lurch and the ship was airborne.

"With Ice-Jock flying we're as good as gone," Zuckless said, before running in the direction Ice-Jock had disappeared.

"Well, are we going to sit here all day or are we going to get a look at our first spaceship cockpit?" Michael asked.

"I wouldn't mind seeing what that citadel looks like now," Edward said.

"Then, what are we waiting for, let's go!" Kate said, and the four of them left the car and followed Zuckless and his Droid companion.

***

"Zaxtooum, the Citadel has been destroyed, nothing survived!"

"My elite guards?"

"Eight limbs managed to carry the three women to a ship and escape, he is waiting to dock with us now, I'm afraid the twins were too slow to escape," Commander Laytoo finished.

He had been ordered to prepare the escape shuttle the moment Zaxtooum had discovered the human's plans to destroy the reactor. Commander Laytoo was not disappointed that Zaxtooum had decided to turn and run. He actually respected the decision, after all, when you know you're going to lose a fight why stay and lose. Better to leave so you can fight future battles, and since the citadel was no longer needed why try and save it.

"Send a shuttle into orbit of Autotron, with orders to wait for a day before searching the remains of the citadel."

"What do you hope to find?" Commander Laytoo asked, realising too late that he had stepped out of line.

"Do not worry yourself," Zaxtooum said, looking at the tense Commander, "you would not know that the twins could survive such destruction. They will be waiting to be picked up."

"But how?"

"Simple, their molecular structure is so dense that it would take a lot more than a small explosion to damage them. They may be slow but they have strength never seen before and a body almost indestructible."

A young alien Lieutenant walked up to the Commander and Zaxtooum,

"Commander, we have a ship on our sensors."

"Eight limbs?"

"No Sir, it's…"

"Ice-Jock!" Zaxtooum finished.

***

"Sensors are showing another ship, No, two ships, Vectors show they must have left the planet right before we did," Zuckless said, as he continued to check the vast array of instruments in front, to the side and above where he sat in his co-pilot seat.

"Zaxtooum," Ice-Jock said, "Well I'm not letting him get away. Kate, your hot with guns, why don't you take a seat in a gun-turret, I'll get you nice and close."

"I'll take the other one," Michael said, who'd always wanted to be in a real dogfight in space.

"After seeing that crater, that used to be a citadel, I thought this was all over." Sally said, checking the restrain straps of her seat.

"I'm still trying to get use to this artificial gravity. Ice-Jock is there anything we can do."

"Just hold on tight and enjoy the ride." Ice-Jock increased the ship's speed and started to close the distance to the enemy, which seemed to be running for cover behind the planet's small moon. Moments after he had increased speed the com-system buzzed. Zuckless met Ice-Jock's confused look.

"What is it?" Sally asked.

"It appears Zaxtooum wants to talk" Zuckless answered. "Think he wants to surrender?"

"I doubt that," Ice-Jock said, "but there's only one way to find out."

Pushing a few switches Ice-Jock opened a channel to the incoming signal. A small screen, at the base of the viewpoint blinked on and the image of Zaxtooum was revealed.

"I'm impressed Ice-Jock, you actually managed to destroy my citadel. It's a shame you went through all that effort for nothing. Since it's already provided me with an army of more than sufficient size to win this war." Zaxtooum said, his face somehow managing a smile out of his contorted features.

Before a reply could be made, Zaxtooum turned his attention to Edward and continued.

"You are quite impressive for a human, defeating my elite guard, surviving a powerful acid, not to mention escaping from a Dragnoor. I could use an ally like you."

"Forget it."

"Well, in that case, when I've won this war I'll have to dissect you to find out how your powers work. Your friends included, though, you are the most interesting subject."

"You won't win, your experimenting is about to come to an end," Ice-Jock said.

"It's a shame you won't be around to see how wrong you are," Zaxtooum said, "Catch me if you can, Ice-Jock."

The COM screen suddenly went blank and hissed with static until Zuckless switched it off.

"The two ship's have ducked and are still heading for the moon," he said.

"He won't get far," Ice-Jock said.

"I can't get any readings, we're being jammed," The Droid said, "this is most likely a trap."

"I don't like this." Sally said.

"It doesn't Matter, we're still going to take Zaxtooum out, even if it's the last thing we do," Ice -Jock said, continuing the pursuit.

The small white/grey moon soon filled the viewpoint as Ice-Jock used the gravity to sling shot faster round and bring Zaxtooum's ship into range. Only Zaxtooum's ship had gone. There was only the emptiness of space on the other side of the moon.

"Where'd he go?" Zuckless said, "He was too close to the moon's gravity to jump to hyperspace."

Before anyone could answer lights and buzzers started to go on and off in the cockpit, everything seemed to go crazy, only Ice-Jock managed to keep his concentration as he performed an emergency double back spin, turning everyone's stomach and narrowly avoiding two missiles.

"That was close," Sally said.

"Where did they come from? The surface?" Edward asked, feeling helpless.

"Eh, guys, girls, maybe someone would like to look out the back and tell me I'm seeing things," Michael said, over the intercom, "I'm seeing a lot of spacecraft out there."

Ice-Jock turned the ship to face the enemy, which filled the surrounding emptiness of space.

"You're not seeing things," Edward said, looking at the armada.

"Why did I have to be right?"

"They must have circled the moon," Zuckless said, motionless.

"Sensors are working again," the Droid said, "and according to the sensors we have ten thousand seven hundred and fifty small drone fighter craft and one four kilometre long warship out there."

"They're attacking, we'll be in range in a minute," Zuckless said.

"Can we run," Sally asked.

"No," Ice-Jock replied, but gave no reason.

"Ice-Jock, those ships are drones, if we take out the main communications tower on the warship we should buy enough time to escape. Without the control brain the drones won't be able to concentrate the attack," Zuckless said.

"Zuckless, we have to go through that lot to reach the mother ship," Michael said.

"Wouldn't it be easier to simply escape," Sally asked, "without going for the mother ship."

"If you think we can fight our way to the enemy's heart, we should be able to fight our way out," Michael added, backing up Sally.

"Thirty seconds," Zuckless said, waiting for a decision to be made.

Ice-Jock made it by increasing speed into the enemy swarm,

"If we leave now, this armada will be able to attack at full force, the alliance won't have time to pull the necessary ships back to defend, so, we have to slow them down before we leave."

"All com frequencies are jammed, we can't warn anyone that way," The Droid said, "we have to get back."

"Ten seconds," Zuckless said, "everyone hold on, it's going to get a little bumpy from here on in."

Ice-Jock applied more speed, pushing the engines to their limit and beyond. Their only hope was to push through the small craft and concentrate on their main target, the mother ship's main communications tower. Four kilometres long, three wide and a kilometre high, the mother ship was an awesome sight. The sensor array and com tower was right at the front of the massive craft and secondary units in its centre on the top of a tower. Bristling with laser and Ion cannons, and covered with a powerful force field the warship alone would have defeated Ice-Jock's small craft. The odds were impossible. With the entire fleet of fighter craft milling around trying to turn his ship into space dust, Ice-Jock didn't need a miracle to win; he needed two.

***

Commander Laytoo watched the view screen and 3-D holographic map from the bridge of Zaxtooum's warship 'Black Rock' Thinking Ice-Jock would turn and run from the armada, he was lost for words as he watched him attack.

"Interesting," Zaxtooum said, also watching, "either Ice-Jock has completely lost his mind or he's brainier than I gave him credit for. It's almost a shame I have to destroy such a good test subject. Still, I can't be too careful. Commander, order the drones to ram the enemy. Should one happen to get on board, have it sabotage the ship and constantly send all its data straight to this console."

"Yes, Master."

***

The ship shuddered with the force of the explosions occurring around it, Ice-Jock seemed to be flying like a mad man to keep them from getting hit, always closing on the warship at the centre of the swarm of drones. Michael and Kate repeatedly fired into the horde of attacking craft, Kate taking careful aim to hit every time. Michael fired wildly, scattering the rest and yelling with delight every so often when he managed, by sheer luck, to hit one, exploding it into a ball of flame.

Edward and Sally felt even more helpless as they watched Zuckless and the Droid frantically direct power from damaged systems trying to keep the ship in one piece. Until there was a sudden hard hit on the starboard side of the ship almost throwing everyone from their seats.

"What the hell hit us?" Ice-Jock shouted over the noise of emergency sirens and alarms.

"We've got a hull breach in the cargo hold, we must have been rammed." Zuckless replied, his hands flying over the controls to seal the cargo hold down.

"Kamikaze aliens?" Edward said.

"I don't know what Kamikaze means but I can tell you now there aren't any aliens flying those ships they are all drones…" Zuckless stopped in mid sentence to look over at Ice-Jock, who finished it,

"Which means we may have an intruder on board."

"That doesn't sound too good, anything vital down there?" Sally asked.

"Only the main power core coupling, destroy that and we're history," Zuckless stated.

"We have to make sure that Drone didn't survive then," Edward said, getting up.

"Won't be easy, I've sealed the doors, the entire cargo bay is open to space, there's a vacuum in there."

"Is there any other way in?" Sally asked, also rising to here feet.

"Yeah, but it means going EVA and doing that in normal circumstances is risky, in the middle of a space battle its suicide," Zuckless said.

"Well, if that's the only option it will have to do, where are the suits?" Edward said.

"Have you been in zero G before?" Zuckless asked.

"No."

"Then its double suicide, you'll never make it," Ice-Jock stated.

"Triple suicide, with that arm of yours," Zuckless said on seeing the blood drip from Edward's hand for the first time, "It's going to take a week to get the blood stains out of my jacket."

"He'll have to make it," the Droid said, "internal sensors are picking up movement in the cargo hold."

"My arm isn't all that bad," Edward assured, flexing his hand, "I'll make it just f…"

"We will make it," Sally interrupted, and before Edward could object she eyed him down, "we go together, I'm not loosing you again, and besides, you will need me."

"You're going to need all the help you can get Ed, those Droids aren't easy to get rid of," Zuckless backed her up. "The suits are in the emergency supply case, one size fit's all and you have thirty minutes of air in each cylinder."

Both Edward and Sally made their way out of the cockpit.

"Good luck, I'll try and keep my manoeuvres as simple as I can, just don't let go," Ice-Jock said as they left.

Edward reached an emergency locker and retrieved the case, which contained the suits. He opened it and handed Sally a suit, sky-blue in colour. They both removed what was left of their clothing to put on the suits. The one-piece suits seemed very baggy at first but once they were on and fastened they became like a second skin, contracting to the individuals body shape, yet they did not restrict movement like Edward had thought. Edward was momentarily in a daze as he eyed Sally's curvy body.

"What about helmets?" Sally asked, seeing Edward's interest.

"Oh, yeah, here we go," Edward said, snapping back into action and handing Sally a biker like helmet.

Again, the helmet was too large for Sally's head but once in place it contracted to the perfect size and shape and automatically sealed itself to the suit. A protective force field shimmered in front of her eyes, giving everything a blue tint. She helped Edward with his air supply after he had helped to fit hers; the flat featureless backpack like box contained two air cylinders and tugged slightly at her shoulders. Once they were ready they both entered the air lock and closed the pressure door. Edward made sure they were both safely clipped in and made a final check on each of their suits before decompressing the chamber and hitting the release for the outer door.

"This is going to feel weird," He said as the door slowly slid open.

Sally heard his voice perfectly through the COM unit, feeling the strange sensation of weightlessness as the small room's gravity unit turned itself off. Looking outside she could see enemy fighters shooting past and firing their laser guns. The small moon and distant planet passed in and out of view randomly and everything seemed to be moving around her in a horrible crazy fusion. She no longer felt as if she was moving, even though she knew Ice-Jock was pulling some pretty hairy and suicidal manoeuvres to keep them all alive. No longer having a sense of up or down and watching the failing mayhem of the battle started to make her feel sick.

"Stop looking out there, keep focused on the metal surface of the ship, it helps," Edward said, somehow sensing Sally's unease, "follow me."

"I'm right behind you," Sally answered, finding that if she concentrated on the ship's hull that she did feel better. She followed Edward and watched his movements, copying as closely as she could. They slowly moved over the outside of the hull, using what handholds they could find, Edward clipping more safety clips to strong locking structures as they went.

Without warning a laser blast hit the ship's hull only a mere meter away from them, the blast was so intensely hot that even in the freezing void of space Sally could feel the metal she held, and the left side of her suit, which had faced the blast, suddenly heat up. She shouted in pain as she let go of the ship, her hands being burnt through the suit by the hot metal, which started to cool again as the heat dispersed over the hull. Sally now found herself floating in the void of space, but before she could grab back on to the hull, the ship dropped away from her. She screamed out as she suddenly found herself being dragged along by her safety cord at its maximum length.

"Sally! Sally! Are you OK?" Edward asked over the COM, he had also burnt his hands but had somehow managed to hold on. It had happened too quickly for his invincibility to be of any use.

"Just get me back! Sally shouted into the COM unit, her voice filled with fear as she hung helplessly on the end of the line. Being in zero G Edward found that pulling Sally back was effortless. Still, once she was back on the hull it took her a full minute before she had the courage to let go of Edward and hold the ship's hull once more.

"Do you want to go back," Edward asked, concerned.

"No, we have a job to do, besides, we've got this far," Sally said, slowly calming herself down.

They continued over the ship's hull, Sally staying much closer to Edward. She noticed movement to her left and turned to see Michael waving to her through the dark glass dome of the gun port, before continuing his wild shooting. His mischievous grin had cheered her up a lot. They reached the site of the collision, a gapping hole, some two meters across; a small part of the alien craft was entangled with parts of the hull and superstructure of Ice-Jock's ship. It was not hard to miss, it could be seen where the atmosphere of the cargo hold had peeled back the hull as it escaped into the void, the collision had generated enough heat to melt the metal and blacken it with fire fuelled by the escaping atmosphere. The metal had only been molten for a few moments; the freezing void of space had quickly frozen it again. Edward grabbed a bent piece of hull metal and looked into the hole, not surprisingly it was pitch black. A little light flashed inside at random intervals when the ship's movement occasionally turned enough to face the hole towards either the sun, the planet or the small moon.

"Let's go in," Edward said and pulled himself forward with part of the bent metal hull. Every action has an equal and opposite reaction. As Edward pulled on the metal it showed that it was not as strongly attached as it looked and broke away from the ship. Edward didn't drift far but when the ship did a sudden dive towards the moon it left him behind until his safety cord went taught.

"Edward!" Sally screamed, in fear of his life.

"Calm down, just pull me in as I did for you," he replied.

As Sally reached out for Edward's safety line the ship turned again and a sharp piece of metal cut through the fine cord. Sally looked up or at least up for her; scanning the surrounding space she could no longer see Edward. He was gone! All she could get from the COM system was static so she turned the COM system off and almost died again inside.

Before, she had lost Edward and taken it as the end. She had never loved someone like this, never this intense or true. Without Edward she couldn't go on, even though they had only known each other for such a short time. It had been Michael then who had convinced her to go on. This time wasn't quite the same, Edward had returned to her from seeming death before, a small voice at the back of her mind somehow convinced her that he would again. With this small hope Sally pulled herself back into perspective. She had a job to do or they would all die. Looking down into the darkness of the cargo hold she concentrated on her task. Turning on a torch she found on the suit's utility belt she pushed herself over the side of the hole and floated down to the floor landing next to the car, which had thankfully been strapped down. She noticed movement to her left and was suddenly filled with fear, realising the dangers of her task for the first time. She was alone, in almost complete darkness, with no gravity and no weapon and she had an unknown droid in the hold with her, programmed to kill.

***

Michael shouted with joy as another enemy fighter exploded within his sights.

"That makes seven," he said aloud.

"No, that's six," Kate said over the COM.

"I didn't think you were counting."

"Well, I am now, since you want to keep a record, I thought I'd make sure it was fact not fiction."

"I don't see what difference it makes," a voice said, inside his mind.

"It makes a difference to me," he said.

"You know, if I weren't telepathic as well you wouldn't be making much sense."

"Would you rather I replied like this?"

"Yes we would," two female voices said in his mind.

"Because me talking...no...telepathically communicating like this gives me one hell of a headache. It's like having a hangover but without the great night before."

"There's no difference, you never remember the night be..." Kate telepathically said.

"What the ..." Michael interrupted so powerfully that he gave both Kate and Blue a slight headache.

"What?" Blue said, in Michael's mind

"What? Kate shouted, over the ship's COM, the same time as Blue.

Michael heard and felt the word before he answered, *"Edward just passed outside, Sally's with him.* Hey! What are you doing out there?" He said, waving to Sally.

Though he knew she wouldn't hear him. The jamming meant communication not hard wired was impossible. The EVA suits had a fine wire connecting them, and so were not connected to the ships internal COM. Still, he watched Sally turn to him and saw her face brighten considerably behind the shimmering force field of her helmet.

"They must have one hell of a reason to be out there," Kate said, over the COM.

Michael started shooting again, "I hope so, this isn't the time for a romantic stroll at night."

Another fighter fell into his target crosshairs to be silenced by Michael's continuous fire.

"Yes!" he shouted, "Seven, right?"

"Right."

***

"Sensors in the hold are now detecting a life sign, we might just come through after all." Zuckless said.

"Wait a minute, what do you mean 'a life sign' there should be two," Ice-Jock noted.

"Something must have happened," the droid sobbed, "they should have both made it."

"Calm down, I need you, whoever made it will find it impossible to fight a droid in zero G, we have got to get the cargo hold artificial gravity back on line and I'm going to need your help, OK?" Zuckless said, facing the droid.

"Yes," she simply replied.

"Just don't start crying, we can't afford to have you short circuit."

"She can cry?" Ice-Jock said, pausing at the controls of the ship. Which was quite fortunate, as two drones had anticipated the end of the manoeuvre. They would have destroyed the ship there and then had Ice-Jock pulled up. Instead the ship carried on round the loop a second time, due to the distraction, and the two enemy drones had destroyed each other.

"I don't know, she's made so many modifications to herself that I don't even think she's a proper droid anymore, but this isn't the time to find out."

"Hey, guys, who changed the plan, we're not travelling towards the warship anymore," Michael's voice sounded over the COM unit.

"Sorry," Ice-Jock said, snapping back into action, "just got distracted for a moment, we're back on course now. Kate, you'll soon be in range but I can't guarantee a clear shot."

"Just tell me what to hit and I'll hit it," Kate said, wondering why she could no longer sense Edwards's presence. She could feel everyone's but his.

***

Edward drifted alone in space. The ship was a great distance away already, rendering the small COM unit on his suit useless. He had a good forty, forty-five minutes of air left but that wasn't what concerned him. Sally would now have to face the droid alone and he feared for her life. He turned to see a small five-meter long drone ship head towards him on a collision course and knew he may have a temporary invincibility, but his space suit didn't. He glanced down at the metal hull plating still held in his hand and decided to let physics save his life. The same physics which had put him in this predicament in the first place. Throwing it with all the strength he had, he sent the metal plating spinning away and himself in the opposite direction, the ship passed harmlessly between the two.

"Ah," Edward said, as he realised a small error in his plans, he was now caught by the planets gravity and was hurtling towards it with increasing speed.

"So much for that idea."

He just hoped his temporary invincibility would last long enough for him to pass through the planet's atmosphere and survive the impact when he reached the ground. Otherwise there wouldn't be anything left of him, just a big hole.

***

Sally moved her torchlight slowly around the room. She held on to a piece of torn metal to keep her from floating uncontrollably. Something red sparked to her left; she shone the light beam towards it and onto a flat piece of metal, reflecting her own image. As she moved the light away something else quickly came into view in the reflective metal. Moving like lightening she twisted away from the attacking droid. She wasn't fast enough in the zero G and felt something tear into her arm, slashing it open lengthways. Sally screamed in pain and fell into a dead spin unable to control her movements. Blood trailed in her wake from the wound until the self-sealing space suit did its work. She slammed into the cargo hold bay wall and somehow managed to grab hold of a pipe to stop her motion. Looking across the hold she could make out parts of the droid in the flashing light of the still tumbling torch. Four, two meter long, doubly jointed, legs hung like a spiders from a shoebox size body. An arm extended from each side, giving it four in total, each with three joints and a meter and a half long. The head, the size of a small fist, sat upon a whip like neck. Three eyes glowed like embers of a fire. Sally found it to be the most hideous thing she had ever seen. The spider like droid started to glide towards her, propelled by small air jets, mounted on each of its limbs. The droid looked designed for almost any environment, including zero gravity. Sally felt frozen to the spot, unable to move due to the incredible pain in her arm and the fear of the approaching droid. She knew all too well that there was no hope for her, especially in zero G. The gap closed and the Droid reached out with its front arm, which ended in dagger like fingers of metal, towards Sally's neck. The four-fingered hand started to close to crush her neck.

Gravity returned.

It was so sudden that she fell away from the droid before the kill could be made. She fell up, hitting the floor; she came out of her roll and ran. The droid had no time to compensate and crashed to the metal floor, head first, right where Sally had landed but she was already on the far side of the cargo hold. With the gravity came friction, with friction Sally could use her great speed more effectively. She looked back to the droid and hoped the fall had destroyed it but did not let herself relax for she knew it would take more than a small two-meter fall. The droid righted itself and stood, almost three meters high with its whip like neck fully extended.

It attacked!

Sally was faster and dodged, diving between its legs and tripping the droid up. As the droid righted itself a second time Sally grabbed a piece of broken metal pipe and struck the droid in the face with all her strength. The head snapped back on its neck but no damage was done. The head just snaked about and looked at her from between its legs. Sally was momentarily taken by surprise and in that moment the droid attacked again. This time the attack connected. Sally felt the wind knocked out of her as she flew backwards and into the cargo bay wall. She slumped to the ground dazed and as she focused on her surroundings again she could see the droid start to charge at her. She screamed in fear as she tried to rise and run. The screams became those of pain as she fell back down, her left leg bent at an impossible angle. She still held the pipe in her hand and raised it towards the droid, in a last desperate bid to defend herself. She was in Lady Luck's hands that day for she managed to raise the pipe just enough to spear the droid's small body. The other end of the pipe had passed through her shoulder and into the metal wall behind. Sparks flew from the droid's wound and the metal shoebox of a body exploded. All the limbs of the droid were sent in opposite directions, spreading all over the cargo hold. The body was reduced to small sharp red-hot pieces of shrapnel, which went everywhere. Sally could only wish she were not so close as millions of metal fragments struck and entered her body. The pain was overwhelming and darkness soon took hold.

***

Ice-Jock's ship danced around, dodging and weaving through the enemy fighters, all the time getting closer and closer to the massive warship. They were then in range of the warship's weapons, which came alive, lighting the surrounding space with a beautiful yet deadly display.

"Wow!" Michael exclaimed, "Looks like there're going for a bit of overkill."

"At least there're hitting their own ships as well," Kate said.

"Only the ones close by, Ice-Jock shouldn't we be in range with our guns as well?" Michael asked, over the COM.

"Unfortunately the warship has weapons with a much greater range than us, the good point is that their weapons are for targeting much larger ships."

"They can still kill us if they hit." Zuckless said.

"Yes," the Droid said, triumphantly, "artificial gravity back on line in the cargo hold."

"Good work."

"Kate, I'll have you in range in about twenty seconds, Michael, add your fire to Kate's, to weaken the shield over the targets." Ice-Jock said.

"That's a big ship, where do I shoot?" Michael asked.

"I'm painting the areas in yellow for you on your targeting computer," Zuckless said, "they will go red when you are in range."

"I hear you."

"At least you can't miss this ship, not as close as we are." Kate giggled.

"Ten seconds." Zuckless said.

"Hey, I'm getting better."

"Almost there," Ice-Jock said and dived the ship between two oncoming laser blasts. Kate watched the target and aimed, setting the gun to full power. The target turned red and Michael sent shot after shot towards the target. The shield absorbed the energy, turning redder and redder as it tried to dispel the onslaught. Kate paused; her mind link with Sally was suddenly broken as if it had never existed.

"Sally's in trouble, she's dying," She said, over the COM.

"Kate, we can't do anything right now, just fire the guns, we can't last much longer," Ice-Jock said.

Kate had known Sally for only as long as Edward, he had developed a great love for the young woman and Kate had become good friends with her.

"She is losing life while you pause; act now and you will have more time to reach her."

Kate took a deep breath and let it out, along with her tension and worry.

"Thank you," Kate said, to Blue, with her mind.

Kate pulled the trigger.

The shields were much more weakened now, with Michael's continuous shooting, as soon as Kate added to his efforts the shields collapsed. While Michael continued his assault, with the laser guns, Kate switched to missiles and sent three true to their mark. The explosion destroyed the communication and sensor array of the warship.

Nothing happened to the enemy fighters.

"Now what?" Michael asked.

"We still have the back up system to destroy remember, I'm heading over there now." Ice-Jock said and altered course, rolling the ship through a corkscrew manoeuvre along the belly of the beast.

***

On the ship's bridge Commander Laytoo approached Zaxtooum.

"They have destroyed our main sensor array and communications tower, should they destroy the secondary…"

"They won't." Zaxtooum interrupted, "intensify weapons fire around the secondary array."

"But their ship is too small for the weapons to lock on."

"Commander, we only need one laser to hit and that ship will be destroyed. Fill the space surrounding the array with weapons fire and the odds are decidedly in our favour."

"Should I command the drones to pull out, we have sustained great losses already, many under our own fire."

"No, Commander, they will increase the odds further in destroying Ice-Jock and his ship. Better to lose half the fleet in his destruction than the entire fleet in his succeeding to destroy that communications tower. He must not be allowed to succeed, whatever the cost."

"I understand, my Lord."

***

"Wow," Michael said, as lasers passed through space, around him, "Ice-Jock, this second target is not going to be easy."

"Destroying that first tower must have hurt him, a lot, he's throwing everything he has at us."

"We're not going to make it, are we?" Kate asked.

"I'm impressed we made it this far," Ice-Jock said, making fine course adjustments, not wanting to dodge one laser and fly into another. He had never flown this hard in all his life.

"Hey, guys, I said this wasn't going to be easy but we can do this, I'm locking all my missiles together and sending them all to the shields. Kate, you do the same and fire on target, three seconds after me. Ice-Jock, as soon as Kate fires get us the hell out of here as fast as you can."

"That will use all our remaining missiles, if it fails to knock out the communications tower we won't be able to have a second shot at this," Zuckless said.

"I know, but I doubt we'd survive for a second shot, we have to blow this thing now."

"He's right." Ice-Jock said, "We're almost there, ten seconds and you're at maximum firing range,"

"Michael, if we don't get through this I..."

"Tell me later Kate, we'll make it."

"At least someone thinks so," Blue said.

"I'm always the optimist."

The ship corkscrewed around oncoming lasers and still managed to find the space to duck and roll away from the missiles, being fired at it from behind by the drone fighter craft. Michael watched his targeting bracket turn red, held steady for a full second, and then fired all seven missiles at his target. He watched them streak away, followed by Kate's, exactly three seconds later. The ship suddenly pulled up and away from the warship, at its fastest possible vector, denying Michael the sight of the explosion. The first he knew to be his, destroying the shields protecting the communications tower. The second blast was Kate's missiles, fired straight and true to the tower itself. Because of the vacuum in space he couldn't hear the explosions and at the angle the ship was flying away he couldn't see them. The first indication he had that they had succeeded was to witness five-drone ships self-destruct.

"Did it work?" Kate's voice came over the COM.

"Yeah, better than I hoped." He answered.

"Trust Zaxtooum, he's built all his drones to self destruct the moment he can't control them." Ice-Jock said.

"Doesn't want anyone using them against him." Zuckless added.

"Hey, guys, the warship is pulling away," Michael noted, " we did it."

"Ice-Jock, we need to land back on the planet, Edwards down there and we need to get to Sally fast!" Kate said, un-strapping her harness and leaving the gun compartment.

"How did Edward get back to the planet?" Ice-Jock asked, as Michael entered the cockpit, Kate not far behind.

"He threw a piece of hull plating and got caught by the planet's gravity."

"Let me guess, he needs clothes again, his space suit having burnt up in re-entry." Michael said, shaking his head.

"Well his suit wasn't completely destroyed, but your more or less correct."

"We'll be back on the planet in a few minutes, the warship has already entered hyperspace."

"What, no message, I thought Zaxtooum would be gloating that he'd be back." Michael said.

"Oh, don't worry, he will be, he just knows that we already know he'll be back. Probably doesn't want us gloating at him that we won."

***

Edward watched Ice-Jock's ship come in for landing, close to a crater, which he had made when he had hit the planet. His temporary indestructibility had lasted for the duration of his fall and landing. He had started to fall unconscious as he had come down and he was still very weak from all the effort he had expended. He now had a very good idea of his limits. The ramp lowered and Kate came running out, not Sally.

"Where's Sally?"

"She's still in the cargo hold, but the door has jammed inside and the cargo hold ramp won't lower. Edward, she's dying."

Edward was on the move like lightening, not stopping at the ship, he jumped up on to the hull and ran over it to reach the hole created by the collision. Dropping down, he scanned the room and spotted Sally, sat up against a wall, pinned by a piece of metal pipe and covered in blood. Running to her side he kicked away a piece of droid, which still twitched with power. He was at her side in moments.

"Sally," he said, a tear forming in his eye, as he felt for a pulse. She was still alive but only just.

He checked her main wound before pulling the pipe from her body. She was covered in so many small cuts that no Matter how he picked her up her blood found a way on to him and what remained of his space suit.

"Don't die, Sal, don't die."

He approached the cargo bay door as a snake like piece of metal dropped from above and suddenly wrapped itself around his neck. A small fist sized head, with three red glowing eyes, faced him, as the metal tightened around his neck. Still holding Sally with one arm he grabbed the metal snake with the other hand and yanked it from his neck, pulling it apart, as he did so. Bits of metal fell to the floor as he continued to look the remainder of the droid in the face.

"Zaxtooum, I'll be coming after you!" Edward said, to the droid before crushing the head to smithereens in his hand. He continued to the cargo bay door and pulled it open with his great strength.

"Where's your medical facility?"

"This way," Zuckless said, he, Michael and the droid had been trying to open the door from the outside and at first thought they had succeeded when it opened.

***

Sally woke, her body numb, yet warm. She looked up and saw Edward looking down at her and she smiled.

"How are you feeling?" Edward asked, smiling back and stroking a few strands of blonde hair out of her face.

"A bit strange, actually," she replied, her voice soft and quiet, "how long have I been out?"

"Three days."

"Three days," she repeated, a little shocked, "did we win?"

"We won, actually you woke up with perfect timing."

"I did, why's that?"

"We're just coming up to Earth, you'll be able to watch our approach, if you feel up to it, that is?"

"I don't think I can move, how bad was I?"

"You almost died Sal, the medical facility on board helped us to stabilise your condition and remove all those splinters of metal, but it was your own body that did all the healing really. We discovered you have a powerful healing factor, many times faster and more powerful than any other human does. It's probably why you feel strange right now. A few more days and you'll be fully recovered, if still a little weak."

"So much has happened to us, so much has changed, do you think we'll be able to carry on with our lives?"

"I don't see why not. Ice-Jock and Zuckless have agreed to keep our powers secret. When we get back to Earth, they plan on going after Zaxtooum. Michael and I are thinking of building our own ship and following, should they find any leads."

"Not quite what I had in mind, but I think I'll be able to cope with it."

"Glad to hear it. You, Kate, Michael and myself, we only have each other, all our families and friends are back in the past."

"Don't remind me, I haven't actually thought about it until now."

"Well, Michael has, and he's created a new motto for us all. 'Death comes hard, not to the dying but the one's who continue to live."

"Makes sense in a strange way, I suppose."

"Well, he is also hopeful of finding a way back, you know how he is."

"Hey, this conversation is getting too sad for my liking, I want to look forward, not back and I recall an invitation to see the Earth from orbit, whatever the year, it's still home."

"That it is." Edward said and lifted Sally up from the ship's medical bed and carried her into the cockpit to join their friends, old and new, at the forward viewpoint.

A small blue planet grew in size as they drew closer. Soon it could be recognised as Earth, with the familiar shaped large green, brown landmasses with deep blue ocean surrounding them and white clouds slowly moving over the surface. The moon to their right and the large dominating sun to their left finished the sight perfectly.

"Even after seeing all the pictures and video images I have never seen anything so beautiful before." Sally said, watching as the Earth started to fill the cockpit window.

"The images we've seen before weren't real, just copies. This, This is real!" Michael added.

"It might be a different time, but nonetheless, we're home." Edward said, holding Sally closer to him.

***

A small black spherical probe immerged from hyperspace and proceeded towards a massive warship. The probe had stayed in touch with the droid, XT1338, which had managed to board Ice-Jock's ship. The long-range probe had continually downloaded all information from XT1338 until it had stopped transmitting, after which, it waited until the enemy ship had entered hyperspace before plotting its own course to meet up with the warship. That was three days ago, it now began docking, so it could download its memory on to the ship's system for analysis. Once downloading was complete, the probe's memory was wiped clean and assigned a new objective.

"Commander, probe P33H has finished downloading its memory."

"Understood, I will inform our Lord personally, continue co-ordination of repairs while I'm gone."

"Yes Sir".

Commander Laytoo left the warship bridge and entered the turbo lift, which would take him to Zaxtooum's private chambers and laboratory. He shivered at the thought of Zaxtooum's experiments and hated going in there, but even with the loss of his Lord's robotic fleet, his Lord's first major defeat, Commander Laytoo knew that the safest place was at Zaxtooum's side. The turbo lift stopped and opened on to an immaculate white corridor. The Commander walked to its end, but, as always, could not stop himself from looking through the glass walls on either side. Gross experiments were being performed in small cubicles, visible through the glass. Ten cubicles were on each side of the corridor, though the Commander knew that many more existed, hidden in the ship. Each cubicle contained a different experiment, some with just chemicals being mixed, some with dead creatures being dissected and others with living creatures having various things altered on them. Sophisticated robots were performing all the experiments. Commander Laytoo was glad that no sound accompanied the sights. As he reached the end of the corridor he noticed that the last cubicle, on each side, held one of Zaxtooum's elite guards. The hideous blue skinned woman, if she could still be sexed, was having new arms attached to her upper torso. The arms were slightly lighter in colour and these each split at the elbow, leading to double forearms, each ending in hands. Zaxtooum wasn't just repairing her; he was modifying her at the same time. The other cubicle contained the jade skinned woman, who was still very attractive to look at, but not at that present moment. Laytoo couldn't remember her being injured so she must have been having modifications done. She lay; strapped to a white slab of metal, cut down the middle from neck to stomach. Her skin was pulled back revealing her insides and as Laytoo watched, bones were being removed and replaced with metal ones. He realised, with shock that the naked woman was fully awake and was looking at him. Turning away in disgust at how Zaxtooum seemed to tinker with life in the way a mechanic would tinker with a droid or machine he pressed his hand on the door and entered the moment it opened. He hated coming down here.

Inside the room was dark and cool, this helped ease Laytoo's stomach. Zaxtooum sat surrounded by monitors and computers. From here Zaxtooum could watch and control every experiment being performed.

"I noticed you were admiring my latest work." Zaxtooum said, the chair turning to face Commander Laytoo.

"I thought you only modified damaged work?" Laytoo asked; intrigued to find out why the jade woman was being altered.

"I do, jade was damaged, her bones were broken by that Edward, when he grabbed her. I've managed to monitor and record his strength, he won't break her bones again."

"I'm sorry, I hadn't realised."

"That aside, why are you down here?"

"Probe P33H has returned and the data has been downloaded. Your informed me to let you know as…"

"I remember what I told you," Zaxtooum said, turning to a monitor not currently in use, "let's see what we have."

Zaxtooum viewed the battle between the female called Sally and XT1338 with great interest, making mental notes on her techniques and powers, so he could modify his elite guards accordingly. When the battle had ended not much else seemed to be happening, so he quickly scanned the data until he almost reached the end. The male, known to his friends as Edward, almost filled the monitor with his face, he spoke,

"Zaxtooum, I'll be coming after you!"

"I'll be waiting." Zaxtooum said as the monitor went black.